MW01656900

MATTERS MOST MACABRE

By
Tylor James

Cover design by Greg Chapman.

ISBN: 9798722872258

The author, too, is purely coincidental.

Praise For . . .

Weirdsmith: Issue One

"In the space of these two stories, Tylor James puts the readers through an emotional wringer. Starting with a Corman style, radioactive body horror that is genuinely gruesome and highly chilling, Mosquito Summer left me wheezing on the floor holding my guts after the last line. Whereas the gentle lyricism of Old Dance Hall left me full of sorrowful nostalgia that was once Rod Serling's stock and trade. Be warned, if you pick this Weirdsmith up, you're likely to find yourself hunting down everything else Tylor James has written."

--- Jasper Bark, author of 'Quiet Places', 'Stuck On You and Other Prime Cuts', and 'Way of the Barefoot Zombie'.

"An assured, accomplished debut issue . . . "

--- DS Ullery, author of 'Highway 181' and 'Beyond Where the Sky Ends'.

Praise For . . .

Daydreams of the Damned: Tales of Horror & Oddity

"With a brisk, snappy style, James leads readers through a series of bizarre, always compelling and frequently gruesome tales. Horror fans across the spectrum should find a lot to love here."

--- DS Ullery, author of 'Highway 181' and 'Beyond Where the Sky Ends'.

"Unnerving characters, witty, wrenching plots, bizarre and unpredictable endings. Before you read these stories, write your will giving away any tranquility, composure, or boredom in your possession!"

--- Jack Ontair, poet, author of 'Ashes & Wine' and 'Sunburst Woman'.

Acknowledgments

A special thank you to the *Willow River Writers* for their continual editorial support and critique throughout the writing of this book. They've improved this work tremendously. Among them are such luminous talents as, Jeanne Green, Linda Koch, Pam Fricke, Sherry Gergen, and Chuck Rang.

I came to this group several years ago as a young writer, having no inkling at all as to how to compose decent fiction. Chuck, especially, pulled me aside early on and informed me about my terrible habit of using too many adjectives and adverbs (a common affliction among novices).

For these learning experiences, I am indebted to the group.

Contents

INTRODUCTION

I never know what to say in these things. So, bear with me. Ready? Here goes.

I, and I alone, wrote the strange and macabre tales you are about to read, and no, I won't give you some damned pretentious cliché about the 'stories writing me'.

Because that would be a lie.

I wrote these stories by the sweat of my brow, the grinding of my teeth, the plunder of my hands. I composed them by biting my fingernails, guzzling black coffee, and spending hundreds of hours at my iPad keyboard (or my trusty ol' Royal typewriter, whenever I needed to get back into the 'creative groove' of things).

Most importantly, these stories were written because I needed to write them. To be happy, to stay sane, to make the heart sing.

At roughly 60,000 words, my heart sings to you now . . .

Well past the witching hour, when all is dark . . .

And I feel there is someone --- or something --- behind me.

'The Muse', some call her. She comes to me, on rare occasions. Most of the time, however, I have to come to her. It's a matter of sitting down and simply writing. Committing words to paper. Letting the heart sing on its own accord, even on days when it insists on merely croaking the melody.

Come to think of it, maybe there's no such thing as 'the Muse' after all. Maybe it's just us --- mere mortals attempting our best to create something authentically fantastic. Something that will outlast ourselves.

Except now, I can see there is something behind *you*, too . . .

Oh, wait! Never mind.

Nothing there, after all.

I must be seeing things again.

With this most bizarre, grotesque, and surprising collection of my short stories to date, I hope that you, gentle reader, will begin seeing things too.

Such 'things' are matters of the heart, of course . . . *matters most macabre*.

All my best,

Tylor James.

MATTERS MOST MACABRE

By
Tylor James

THE DAY THE STORIES DIED

Eugene McAllister was a bestselling author until the morning he awoke to discover his imagination vanquished. After five hours' frustration and hardly a word typed, he lay his head upon the keyboard in defeat. Switching to pen and paper, he hoped a change in medium would produce some creative sparks. He ended his writing session weeping over the notebook, wetting the thin blue lines into wavy blurs. With dreadful certainty, Eugene knew the career he'd forged for himself was over. There were simply no stories left inside him.

Eugene relayed this over the phone to his literary agent of the past twenty years.

Maynard Collins asked, "Are you an ignoramus?"

"The hell kind of question is that?" Eugene frowned, flummoxed by Maynard's callous tone. He sat in his robe on the living room couch.

Maynard scoffed. "Turn on the news for God's sake. You're probably the only person on Earth who doesn't know."

"Know what?"

"Turn on the news."

Eugene reached for the remote on the coffee table and flipped on CNN. Anderson Cooper reported the worldwide catastrophe that had occurred overnight. "All of the stories on planet earth have disappeared," Cooper reported, his azure eyes welling with tears. "Vanished into, into thin air. This is very strange, folks. I don't know . . . how else to explain it."

Eugene learned from multiple incoming reports that very few books remained --- only instruction manuals and how-to books. Yet there no longer existed an Epic of Gilgamesh, Rigveda, Iliad, or Odyssey.

No Bible, Torah, Koran.

No Shakespeare, Voltaire, Dante.

No Shelley, Dickenson, Poe.

No Twain, Faulkner, Steinbeck.

No Bradbury, Asimov, Ellison.

No Vonnegut, Plath, Le Guin.

No King, Grisham, Gaiman --- No nobody.

All the stories --- *Poof!* A disappearing act utterly without charm. There were no more tales to be read. None to be told. For no one could remember any, and like Eugene McAllister, nor could anyone create any. Humankind had gone to sleep, ancient and modern lullabies alike hummed into their ears and stored in their minds, only to awake with bankrupt imaginations. All the libraries, public and private, became empty shelves coated with dust --- as if the books had never been there at all.

The internet featured no stories or fictions of any kind either. Even Eugene's Microsoft Word files had been erased, along with everything he'd stored on various USB keys.

Maynard's voice seemed to drift from out of a fog.

"So, you see," he said, "no one can write anymore, because no one can imagine."

"This is a hoax." Eugene stared at his TV in disbelief.

"Oh really? Just a minute ago you were sobbing into my ear about being done for. You mean to say you've got a new story in mind?"

"Well . . . no, but surely this can't be---"

"Tell me," Maynard interrupted. "In summation, what is Bradbury's classic novel *Fahrenheit 451* about?"

Eugene opened his mouth, then promptly shut it. He clenched the phone in his hand, wanting to crush it.

"Easy, partner," Maynard warned. "I can smell your neurons cooking from here."

Eugene released a shaky sigh. "Christ, Maynard. I love that book! It's one of my favorite novels."

"I like it too," Maynard replied. "Except I can't tell you why or what the hell it's about. Nobody can. How about the Bible? Can you tell me any of the stories in there?"

Wind whistled into one of Eugene's ears and out the other. A very dim lightbulb went off.

"Well, there's some character named Jesus . . . I think."

"Uh-huh. And what does this Jesus do?"

"I don't know."

"Damnedest thing, ain't it?"

"Yeah," Eugene mumbled. He stared vacantly into the television, watching Cooper's mouth move yet no longer hearing the words. "Damnedest thing."

"What were we talking about again?" Maynard asked, his tone suddenly one of trepidation.

"Not sure," Eugene replied. "You were telling me something about the world. A story of some sort."

"What's a story?"

***

Eugene McAllister may have lost his ability to imagine along with the rest of humanity, but he still understood what a story was. "A story," he told to himself, "has a beginning, middle and end." He floored the gas pedal, determined to get the hell out of the city. A small wayward cottage located on a private lake awaited him. He'd brought along three blank notebooks and plenty of pens. He'd sit down and, God willing, he would write a story.

A story, he told himself, has a beginning, middle and end.

The sun was setting. Wind ruffled his hair through the open window. He felt good, had almost forgotten what'd happened to the world, until he popped his favorite Bob Dylan album into the CD player. The guitar and harmonica came through fine, but Bob's voice was nowhere to be heard. The lyrics were missing. They had been story songs.

Eugene shut off the stereo. Listened to the wind flap the ceiling's loose fabric. The wind had no stories to tell. Neither did he.

My life is over, he thought. Is that a story?

His stomach began to roil, forcing him to pull over. He spewed hot chunks onto the highway. Cars honked as they swerved by. People shouted.

Wiping rancid spittle from his lips, he whispered, "A story has an end, a . . . no. Wait. A story has a, has a . . . Oh, Christ."

His shoulders hitched with sobs, all for the knowledge of some lost preciousness, not knowing what it was or why it was precious.

***

The BP Station offered the usual conveniences: gasoline, Slurpee's, greasy snacks. Yet its magazine and newspaper racks offered little. Eugene picked up a copy of *USA Today*. The headline informed him that the stock market had crashed, although the article itself consisted of merely a few words scattered among columns of grey, tepid space. The writer, apparently, had relied upon literary devices to explain the stocks.

Eugene flipped through *USA Today*, appalled by the mostly blank pages, then slapped it onto the rack.

A young woman with a ponytail rang up his items. Kensy, her name tag read. Her lips smacked with bubblegum.

"Will that be all, Sir?"

"Yes."

"Four bucks even."

He paid cash, trying to smile. She handed him his change without even a flicker of eye contact. Halfway out the exit door, Eugene turned around. "Hey, Miss? Can *you* define what a story is?"

Kensy frowned. Blew out a pink sphere, popped it, and smacked her lips. "No, duh. You think I'm stupid or something?"

Eugene sighed with relief. She knew what a story was. Yes, of course. Everyone knew what a story was for God's sake, except . . . not him. The writer.

"What's a story?" Eugene asked, nervously tightening his grip upon the door bar. "Tell me."

Kensy crossed her arms. "It's a . . . well, I mean. It's kind of, like . . ."

Eugene began to tremble. Please, he thought. *Please.*

The cashier's eyes landed on the issue of USA Today, where he'd left it cockeyed on the rack.

"It's like that headline!" she exclaimed. *'Stock Market Crashes.'* See? That's what a story is. A story is a headline."

She was guessing, Eugene surmised. But she had guessed wrong. Very wrong.

He shook his head, sad for them both, then got back on the road.

***

Earth is round.
Twenty-four hours in a day.
The human body is sixty percent water.

Hunched over his writing desk, Eugene filled four notebook pages with such statements. The cottage smelled of cedar and pine, its ceiling a bare framework of trusses and crossbeams. Spider webs festooned truss to truss. Spider webs festooned his brain, too. Numbing himself with a bottle of *Captain Morgan*, he eyed the notebook wearily.

Statements. Facts. Bare-boned platitudes.

The drab skeletons of language.

Although he couldn't remember what stories were, he was positive they weren't anything like what he'd written. He had easily composed, *'My cottage was built fifty years ago'*, yet found he could not commit pen to paper when trying to explain how the cottage was built or who built it.

Wiping sweat from his forehead, he drew deeply from the bottle, and tried again.

With trembling hands, he scrawled:

I, Eugene McAllister, am a writer.

Networks of synapses, dendrites and neurons boiled beneath his cranium. He pushed himself to compose the next sentence. Another draw from the bottle. His throat burned. He needed to explain, longed to convey *how* he had become a writer, where he'd first been published, what the title of his debut novel was . . .

His pen and the blank page acted like two identical poles of a magnet, each repelling the other. And to think that throughout his life, up until now, the pen and paper had been opposites --- naturally attracted.

The tip of his pen simply would not touch the paper, no matter how forcefully he pressed downward. The pen hovered maddeningly. A perpetual tease.

Not that it would've mattered even if he *had* managed to touch pen to paper. Tears dripped down his cheeks. If asked, he wouldn't even have been able to explain his tears.

Doing so would've required he tell a story. *His* story.

Eugene polished off the rum, then went to bed. On the hazy edge of unconsciousness, a word sprang up out of the pitch dark --- one word, so mysterious, tantalizing, and forbidden.

And the word was . . . *Hemingway.*

Upon glimpsing those three arcane syllables, Eugene fell deeply asleep, his face planted into a pillow as white as the blank page, as dread snow, as a mind vacant and pallor-faced as the moon.

***

Eugene's royalties as a bestselling author provided him ample money, although not enough to retire. Therefore, he kept a side gig --- a profession rendered seemingly useless by the inexplicable plague which had swept the world of its stories.

Eugene was an English professor at Miskatonic University, located in the town of Arkham, Massachusetts.

Monday morning. His clothes were rumpled, and he'd forgotten his tie. He leaned back in the driver's seat, commencing the hour-long drive from his cottage to the university. Turning on the radio, he scanned the stations. The latest facts and figures resounded out of mechanical mouths:

The stock market hadn't just crashed. It'd burned to a crisp.

Suicide numbers had skyrocketed. Half the country was dead --- approximately one hundred and sixty million people.

The *worldwide* suicide number was drastically higher.

Eugene cranked the tuning knob to those ever-amusing evangelical stations. His heart sank as preachers made sobbing renouncements of faith. The book upon which they'd based their religion had disappeared, and no one could remember what it'd said. Another yank of the tuning knob proffered terrible pop songs with disjointed lyrics. That, at least, hadn't changed. Eugene preferred the wind.

Then, with a surge of glee, he remembered the classical stations. Now that was music! Wondrously beautiful orchestras --- all without lyrics, without stories.

The orange dial-needle combed through the channels. Eugene's face fell slack at the buzzing static. Not a note came through.

How could this be? He thought awhile, puzzled. Then it occurred to him even symphonies told stories . . . often grand, cosmic, poignant stories, composed of a dynamic instrumentation of sounds and cadences --- a language all its own.

All of it gone. Not one name of any composer even came to his mind.

They may as well have never existed, whoever they were.

Eugene clenched his teeth and shut off the radio with his fist.

***

Dark half-circles. Eyes within sunken sockets. Mouths half-open with saliva hanging in silver gleaming strands. Eugene stood at the front of the lecture hall, a blank whiteboard behind him. Half the lights were off, as no books required illumination for reading.

Back and forth, he paced. The student body (less than half remained in a hall that on any previous week would've filled no less than two hundred seats), stared up at him with glazed eyes. Young men and women of once brilliant potential --- now dull, insipid cogs in the arteries of the world. They reminded him of dogs.

Stupid dogs.

And he was enraged --- for he knew he was no better.

After twenty minutes wracking his brains, sweeping the linoleum with his shoes like a lunatic, grey hair all unkempt and face pallid, he halted. Frozen there at the front of the hall, *the word* returned to him, as if arising from out of some dark recess of a previous life.

Eugene smiled, stepping closer to his students. The eyes shimmered up, like liquid voids, and he said, almost in a whisper, "*Hemingway.*"

A *magic* word. The eyes unglazed, once again teeming with life. The students turned their heads, exchanging glances as if awakening from a voodoo spell.

Hemingway, yes! *Hemingway!* That tough ol' bastard with his love affairs and bullfights and bone-dry martinis and simple, clean, elegant sentences that brought you deep into the heart of his world. Yes, *that* Hemingway.

Then Eugene's smile sunk like a cannonballed galleon. The eyes, all of them, had glazed over in a second. Jaws slacked. Saliva dribbled. He spun around, picked up a dry erase marker, put its felt tip to the board . . . almost.

They refused to touch. No matter how much he concentrated. No matter how hard he forced his hand.

There, in plain sight of the diminishing student body, Eugene cried long and hard and deep, for he could no longer remember that perfect, magic word.

The lecture ended early.

School was out.

Forever.

***

On the seventh chime, Eugene answered the phone:

“Yeah?”

"Hi, Eugene! It's Valery. How are ya?"

Valery was Maynard Collins’ secretary, incidentally one of the most adorable and wise women Eugene ever met.

"Not doing so hot, actually. Feeling . . . sick.”

"Aww, I’m sorry to hear that, hon." Even in a world half-extinct, Valery’s honeyed tone remained. Eugene drank from a new bottle of rum.

“I’ll be okay. How are *you* doing, Val?”

“I have unfortunate news," she replied. "It's Maynard. He's dead."

Eugene fumbled the rum bottle. He caught it just before hitting the floor, then set it on his desk. His heart pounded, not understanding why. Maynard was dead. Most people were these days. Still, the news was shocking.

"Jesus, Val," Eugene replied. "I'm sorry. How . . . how’d he die?"

"Jumped from his office window."

"*Jesus.*" He closed his eyes, thinking of Maynard’s office ten stories up.

"Who's Jesus?" Valery’s tone was curious.

"Never mind that," he replied, irritated. "Val, why’d he jump? He must’ve been depressed, out of a job? Christ, all of this must’ve taken a toll on him. Hell, I know it’s taken a toll on *me.*"

"Oh, I doubt it," she replied coolly. "Collins Literary Agency is transferring over to non-fiction manuscripts, like everybody else. Maynard had a job, just didn't want it."

". . . I see." Eugene frowned, not liking Valery's cold nonchalance. Not liking it one bit. Her honeyed tone from a few minutes ago now seemed artificial and empty.

"We're focusing on how-to books and technological instruction pamphlets," she informed him. "Say, Eugene honey, think you can write us a how-to pamphlet on assembling a BISSIL AirRam cordless vacuum? There's a market demand for vacuum literature these days. Could mean good money."

"I imagine so." Eugene's voice was low and thick. "Listen, I gotta go."

"Sure, hon. Give me a ring when you come up with some solid non-fiction."

He hit 'end call', then threw his phone across the room in a burst of rage. The screen fractured upon the wall into infinitesimal pieces. Spider webs among the cottage trusses swayed, and the new rum bottle emptied almost on its own accord.

***

Eugene sat in a chair on the front porch. His thousand-yard stare was bloodshot and vacant. Birds twittered in the red dawn sky.

He did not know who he was anymore. No one did.

One's personal history, after all, is a story.

Eugene pondered the sun and the birds. How did each thing get here? How did they form? He only knew birds flew and made noises. He only knew the sun produced heat, kept him alive.

He wetted the cold steel shotgun barrel with his tongue and tasted oil.

For a moment, for one transient eternity, the magic word popped into his mind again, making him extraordinarily happy.

Then Eugene pulled the trigger.

His smile ripped off his face and flew up, up, up into a hundred pieces, rising like red little birds in the frigid morning. The shot rang into the distance, followed by a moment of silence.

Then the birds continued twittering sweet nothings.

The sun also rises, having nothing to tell, save this:

For while dead men tell no tales,
no tales surely make for dead men.

INDEPENDENCE DAY IN HOLEBRIM, TEXAS

Every breath was like suckin' in air with your lips pressed against a furnace vent. Sweat ran constantly under sweltering heat. I was ten years old.

Momma was makin' a Fourth of July dinner and we was all excited about it. Daddy wasn't there, 'cause he hadn't been around since we were babies. Grandpa though, he was there.

Gramps' age was about as high as the heat index. He was a hundred 'n nine, or a hundred 'n ten. We lost count long ago and Gramps couldn't recall nothing. But we *did* know this: Fourth of July, America's birthday, was also Grandpa's birthday.

That was good for us kids. Every Fourth of July meant double the fun. Momma made up the dining table like it was Thanksgiving; cookin' up chicken, stuffing and gravy, mashed potatoes, green beans, corn on the cob; and best of all, big ol' slices of watermelon for desert.

Momma called us all into the house at dusk. We'd been playing 'neath the dead tree outside, pretending we was cowboys and Indians. Lilly, who was youngest, was the Indian. Me and Ricky were cowboys. Ricky got to play

John Wayne 'cause at twelve years old, he was oldest.

From toddler on up, I was taught oldest always got first preference. It was like a reward for years lived or somethin'. I figured that's why Grandpa was so special. Us kids raced each other inside the house.

Momma’s real pretty. She's got bright blue eyes and sandy blonde hair tied up in a ponytail. "Boys?” she said. “Go on and fetch Grandpa. Bring him to the table. And remember, be polite! It's his birthday."

"Yes, Momma," said Ricky, scratching his backside with a slingshot.

"Okay, Momma," I said.

"And Ricky," she said, "put that thing away. You know I don't like it in the house. You end up breakin' things."

"I won't break nothin' with it, Momma," said Ricky. "I'll be real careful and keep it in my back pocket. See? I don't wanna keep it outside, Momma. The weather'll get to it and it won't sling so far."

Ricky pouted. "Oh, fine," Momma said, rolling her eyes. “Lilly?"

My eight year old sister looked up from the table. She had a dolly on her lap and an empty plate in front of her, just waiting for a helpin' of steamin’ chicken and potatoes.

"Yeah, Momma?"

"Come help set the table, sugar."

Ricky and I darted out the kitchen and raced up the stairs.

"Gonna beat you, Donny!" said Ricky, three steps behind.

"Nuh-huh!" I called back, climbing the steps fast as I could. Ricky grabbed the seat of my pants, yanking me. I reeled backward, arms propelling the air, 'till I caught the banister.

"Ha-ha!" Ricky said and zoomed past. Momma shouted from the kitchen to stop rough housin'. Ricky opened the door at the end of the hall. Grandpa's room. We went in.

Grandpa sat where he always sat --- in a wheelchair beside the window. The old man's face was an ancient contour map; a rugged display of hills and valleys, his every wrinkle and crease like rivers and trenches. His mouth hung slightly open. He looked out the window, down onto our dusty driveway, where Momma's Oldsmobile was parked.

Ricky and I stood beside him. He didn't bother saying anything. At his age, Momma said, Gramps had a right not to be social. As I've mentioned, old age had its preferences in our household.

Hell, you can get away with anything when you're old. Even if you shit your pants, no one will blame you. "He's just old," someone will remark. Then they'll close-pin their noses and change your smelly diaper.

Old men are like pruned up old babies. That's what Grandpa looked like to me, sitting before the sunlit window. One pruned up, oversized baby. He smelled plenty ripe too, though I don't think he ever needed a diaper, thank God. If he'd had, I would've been handed the chore of changing it.

"Happy birthday, ya old fart!" Ricky said.

"That ain't funny," I scolded.

"Yeah, it is."

"No, it ain't."

"*Sure* it is."

It was futile trying to reason with him. Ricky thought he could say anything to Gramps' face just 'cause he couldn't hear so well. My thinkin' was that didn't make it right. Ricky grabbed the wheelchair's handlebars. The rims used to be so bright 'n shining, you could see your reflection in 'em. Now they was all rusty with time; compromised by entropy, like I'd learned in science class.

You see, everything gets old and rots. Everything decays. Rusts. Breaks down. That's what entropy is. Scientists say the universe is run by it. That's why ninety-nine point nine percent of species that've lived on this planet have gone extinct. It's also why our sun'll burn out one day, leaving the earth a cold, icy ruin. My ten year old brain was ruminatin' on this stuff while Ricky pushed Gramps into the hallway over to the landing.

I went down the first three stairs, and lifted up the front wheels. I was plenty strong enough to lift Gramps and his chair. The old man was thin as a reed and weighed light as a throw-pillow. As we descended, Ricky jiggled the wheelchair left and right, tryin' to make me lose my grip.

"Stop that!" I said.

Ricky laughed, kept doing it.

"I said stop it, Ricky!"

"Fine, fine, you wuss! I'll stop."

Ricky quit jostling the chair. We was halfway down the stairs when he yanked the chair to the left and right, real violent-like. Gramps tottered in his seat. I lost my grip. The front wheels hit the stairs. Gramps tilted forward dramatically.

"*Oomph!*" Gramps' face collided with my own. Our noses touched. I stared into his dark, time-weary eyes. He didn’t blink.

Ricky howled with hilarity.

"You bastard," I said. "Help me put 'em back in his chair!'

Ricky stifled his giggles long enough to pull back the old man's frail shoulders, setting him into the chair.

"Sorry about that, old fart," Ricky said, patting Gramps' shoulder.

"You're a real asshole, you know that?"

"Watch it, or I'll sling ya!" He liked to launch things at me sometimes. Marbles. Rocks. Hot Wheels. Double-A Batteries. Whatever it was, it usually hurt like hell. I picked up the front of the wheelchair. We got to the bottom.

Ricky wheeled Grandpa into the kitchen. The air smelled of delicious, roasted chicken and potatoes. Lilly and Momma had the table set.

"Thank you, boys," said Momma.

Ricky nodded proudly and sat next to Lilly so he could elbow her in the ribs. Lilly, only eight, returned the jabs no problem. One time she even made Ricky cry. Almost a teenager, and he wailed like a baby. I loved my Sis even more from that day on.

"None 'a that, now," said Momma. She had that stern look in her eyes, the kind that turn her sea blue irises into cold ice-daggers. Ricky quit the elbow-jivin'. "Time for grace," she said. We bowed our heads. Grandpa too. "Bless us, Lord," she smiled, "for these, thy gifts that we're about to receive from thy bounty through Christ, our Lord. Amen."

"AMEN!" Ricky's hands flew to the roasted chicken, ripping off its left leg.

"Ricky Donahue!" Momma shouted, slapping the food out of his hand. "Where's your manners?"

"He ain't got none, Momma," I said.

"Aww, keep quiet, you rapscallion!" Ricky grinned.

Ricky liked that word, rapscallion. He used it on occasion and I thought it sounded funny, so I smiled. "Don't encourage him," Momma told me.

"Sorry, Momma."

Ricky began forking mashed potatoes onto his plate.

"*Ahem,*" said Momma. Ricky dropped the fork with an exaggerated sigh.

"Before we enjoy this wonderful meal I've prepared," she said, "let's watch Grandpa take the first bite. It's his birthday tradition, after all."

"Yeah, you barbarians!" Lilly giggled.

"Thank you, Lilly," Momma said, with a wink. "Grandpa? Would you prefer a bite of chicken, or potatoes?"

Gramps was silent. Ricky nudged him under the table. He leaned ever so slightly toward the bowl of mashed potatoes.

"Excellent choice, Daddy," she said, and scooped a tiny lump of white potato on the end of a spoon. She brought it to his mouth. Gramps wasn't cooperating. She took her index finger and pushed the lump of potatoes inside his mouth.

"Okay," said Momma. "Now everyone can feast."

And feast we did. That meal was melt-in-your-mouth delicious. So delicious, Gramps' fetid B.O. didn't even bother us none. The sunlight through the dining room window waned until gone. People were out there lightin' off fireworks. We couldn't see 'em through the window, but we could hear 'em all right. High-pitched missiles screamed up into the sky, then crackled like a million cellophane wrappers.

My legs kicked and tapped the floor. Lilly and Ricky's, too. We were eager to get outside and launch our *own* fireworks. We hastily cleared our plates. Lilly and Ricky started pickin' up the dirty silverware. Momma stood at the sink, filling it up with soapy water. I went over to Gramps with a napkin, began cleaning his chin of potatoes and corn kernels. It had always been my chore to clean Grandpa up after our meals.

I wiped his lips and picked some gunk off his teeth, when

WHACK!

Something hit Grandpa's chest. A small billow of dust arose off his shirt. A mottled-grey stone sat in his lap. Ricky stood beside the table, returning the slingshot to his back pocket. He smiled. Momma and Sis continued washin' and dryin' dishes, unaware.

I shook my fist. Ricky shrugged nonchalantly, putting the remaining food into the ice box. I pocketed the stone. The fabric of Gramps' yellow, crusty shirt had worn through. I could see his chest underneath. No bruise. No blood. Grandpa never bled or bruised, no matter *what* Ricky did to him.

One time he'd taken a pocket knife to Gramp's right arm, making an incision about five inches long. Gramps never yelled or cried. Just took it silent, like he takes his meals, like he takes the preservative baths Mamma prepares, like he takes everything.

I wheeled Gramps outside. After a while, Momma brought out a large tray of watermelon slices. The evening had grown cooler, but we was still as hot and sweaty as an African safari. Except Gramps, of course. Gramps stunk real bad when it got hot, but he never sweat, just like he never bled. Gramps was John Wayne to me. Real tough and dignified. He endured life with stoic calm.

Ricky devoured two slices of watermelon, then brought out our fireworks. He grinned wildly, Roman candles, firecrackers, and Screaming Meemies all bundled under his arm.

The sky had grown dark now, lit by a pale moon. A few bright stars were out. It all made for another fine Fourth of July in Holebrim, Texas. Lilly helped Momma bring out folding chairs so we could sit out in the half-acre plot of dirt we called a yard.

Ricky organized the explosives, arranging them from least impressive, to most. He danced around like a mad injun.

I brought Gramps over to sit beneath our one, dead tree. The barren branches made shadows in the moonlight. Grandpa's ancient face was white beneath the moon. Although in natural light, his complexion was turquoise.

Lilly and Momma sat in chairs, spittin' watermelon seeds, watchin' Ricky prepare his meager show of half a dozen explosives (it was all Momma could afford). My brother was about as excited as an alley cat doused in gasoline and lit on fire.

"Rick-y! Rick-y! Rick-y!" Momma and Lilly cheered. I stood next to them and watched. Gramps watched over by the tree, to the left of the house. Ricky lit the firecrackers first.

Pop-pop-pop-pop-pop-pop-pop! Wisps of smoke rose into the air. The firecrackers were done in under a minute. Momma clapped.

"Heck of an opener, Ricky," I said, lamely.

"What?" he asked. "Not impressed? Well, you will be!"

He brought out the Screaming Meemies next. They came in one small box. Ricky set it level on the ground, then lit the wick. Orange sparks flitted. Ricky took four steps back.

"Ricky!" Momma shouted. "Step back, *way* back!"

I wished Momma hadn't said that. Ricky was safe now, standing beside us, totally free of personal danger. Dozens of brilliant red, white and blue orbs shot up out of the box, screaming into the Texas night like banshees. My ears prickled. Everyone whooped and hollered.

Soon those were done too. Ricky looked real sad about it. The box lay there, smoking, burnt out. The smoky air stunk with sulfur.

"Shouldn't there be *more?*" Ricky asked.

"Honey, you know these things don't last all that long," Momma replied.

Lilly and I giggled at Ricky's disappointment.

"Shut it, you two, or I'll sling ya both!" Ricky said.

"Nobody will be slingin' nothin', 'cept me!" Momma replied. "And what I'll be slingin' is a belt."

We knew she meant business. Momma's beatings were legendary. Lilly and I ceased giggling. Ricky kicked aside the box, its plastic wrapping mostly burnt away. I thought of the Screaming Meemies. How they rose into the air, all raging bright and loud, then fadin' into the sky, their screams squelched into nothing.

It was entropy. It was everything, running down. The sun. The stars. The fireworks.

Grandpa, too. While I was ruminatin' on these things, Ricky reclaimed his mojo. He was all excited again, jumping up and down. "Oh boy, oh boy!" he said. "And now, for the *big* finish!"

Ricky brought out the Roman candles. They were the sticks you held while balls of fire shot out and made explosions in the sky.

"Ricky, honey," said Momma. "Why don't you let your little brother give it a try first?"

"But Mom!"

"But, nothin'! Has Momma taught you how to share, or hasn't she?"

Ricky pouted. "Yeah, Momma. You have . . ." Then, under his breath, "*god damn it all.*"

"RICKY DONAHUE."

"Sorry, Momma!" He shoved the candle into my face and whispered, "Hope ya blow your face off."

I used the bic lighter and lit it. Red balls of fire shot up into the moonlit sky. The candle vibrated in my hands.

"Oooooh," they said. "Ahhhhh."

Then it was spent. "Lilly's turn!" said Momma.

Ricky hung his head.

"Yaaayyy!" She sprinted over, her yellow dress billowing in a fresh, light breeze. I gave her instructions on how to use the candle. She did it all on her own, no problem.

"That was fun!' she said, dropping the spent candle to the ground.

"Okay, Ricky," said Momma. "Now you can do the rest."

Ricky cheered. The breeze picked up, blowing west. Lilly sat in the chair next to Momma. I stood behind her. Ricky lit another candle. Balls of fire blew this way and that, making Momma nervous.

"Careful now!" she said. "Aim that thing up, hear me? *Straight* up!"

Ricky aimed straight up until the candle was spent. Onto the next one. Then that was done too.

Momma stood, folding up her chair. She thought that was the last candle. Ricky watched her and Lilly pick up the watermelon trays and gather the chairs. A small, ominous smile dimpled his cheeks. I frowned, knowing a thought had crossed his mind. One of the no-good ones. He turned away.

"What a show!" Momma said.

"I loved firing that rocket-stick!" said Lilly.

Ricky lit the candle, pointed it at the dead tree, where Grandpa sat nearby. "Ricky, don't you dare," I yelled, but it was too late.

The wind ruffled my hair. The fireball shot out. Not upward, but towards the tree. I watched the fireball inevitably curve with the wind.

It exploded in Grandpa's face. Momma screamed. Lilly too. I stood there while a shroud of flames enveloped Grandpa's head. Ricky's mouth dropped open. He'd abused Gramps plenty over the years, but he'd only been aiming for the tree.

The candle went off in his hands a second time, launching another red hot fireball. The wind hadn't died. Gramps was hit a second time, this time in the crotch. His pants went up in flames, spreading quickly down his legs and up his shirt.

"Ricky, *no!*" Momma sobbed. Hearing her cries broke Ricky out of his daze. He adroitly shifted the candle upward. It shot up into the night, where it was supposed to. Momma sprinted over to Grandpa.

POP! . . .

POP! . . .

POP! . . .

Ricky stood there like a dumb Grecian column, eyes wide, watching Grandpa burn. The sky was exploding and for once, he didn't care. Lilly stood petrified, her hands pressed against cheeks wet with tears.

Momma knocked Grandpa out of his chair, took off her t-shirt and began smothering the flames. She wasn't wearing a bra. I'd never seen Momma's breasts before. They drooped like udders. "WATER!" she screamed. "FETCH A PITCHER OF WATER!"

The final candle had burnt out. Ricky held it at the sky. I punched his shoulder and said, "Come on! Help!" He shook his head, as if just awakened from a daydream. We sprinted past Momma and our burning Grandad.

A blazing fire engulfed his entire body. Momma beat him with the shirt bunched within her fists. She rolled him in the dirt with her feet, yelping as the fire burned her toes. She was wearing flip-flops.

Ricky and I searched feverishly about the kitchen for the pitcher. Where was the damn pitcher? Jesus God, it had to be somewhere!

"I dunno where it went!" Ricky cried. Then I remembered where it was. I'd brought it down to Lightnin' Crick earlier that afternoon. To make little mud houses. And now Gramps was outside, flesh melting, making a little house of bones.

"Look for a bowl, then," I shouted, not wanting to fess up to having forgotten the pitcher. "Look for the biggest one we got!"

We looked for a bowl. Momma's cries developed into desperate shrieks. Knocking away queer looking jars of chemicals preservatives, I discovered an old, tin bucket under the kitchen sink. We'd used it every Halloween to bob for apples.

"Quick, put it under the tap!" Ricky ordered. I put it under the tap. The bucket filled slowly, slowly.

"HURRRY!" Momma shrieked.

We got the thing half-way full, said good enough. Ricky ran it outside. Water sloshed over the side as he ran. The bucket also had a hole in the bottom. It leaked through kitchen, into the leaving room, onto the porch, into the yard.

Momma's face was buried in her hands. Gramps looked like a giant black turd, set a 'fire. Smelled that way, too.

"Hang on, old fart!" Ricky said and overturned the bucket. Water cascaded, hissing as it soaked him. The flames died. Grandpa lay there, unrecognizable. His flesh, once so well-preserved, was now blackened, charred, smoldering.

I knelt beside Momma, even though she was half-naked.

"Go get Momma a shirt," I said. Ricky disappeared into the house to get it.

Momma sobbed all over me. Snot hung from her nose.

"It'll be okay, Momma," I said. "It was Grandpa's time, is all. Entropy. That's the way of the universe, Momma."

All that came out were crying gasps. Her shoulders hitched. Her eyes watered more than that bucket we brought out. Lilly sat on the porch steps, tears streaming. Ricky, in a rare display of affection, kissed her atop the head. He brought over a clean shirt. Momma wiped her runny nose with the back of her hand, then put it on.

"W-w-why, Ricky," she said, voice quivering. "*Why did you do it?*"

"I didn't mean to, Momma," said Ricky, shaking his head. "Honest, I didn't! I was aimin' for the tree. It was the wind's fault, Momma. That wind . . . well, it got real strong. I wasn't expectin' it, is all."

Momma's response was hotter than the flames that'd burned up Grandpa. Ricky ended up getting a beatin' within inches of his life. Momma even threated to light him on fire, see how much *he* liked it, but never did.

Lilly and I drug Gramps' charcoaled corpse out of our yard, once he'd cooled off some. You could see his skull. The sockets were hollow, and the bone was white as the moon above.

Both of us grabbed a foot and drug him. His shoes had burned clean off. The remaining flesh was black and sticky on our hands. We brought him out into the nearby field. Ricky's screams from Momma's beating danced on the wind.

Oh, the wind, I thought. *That damn wind!*

Feeling it graze my cheek and ruffle my hair only reminded me of the Roman candles. How they exploded into Gramps' face, then onto his crotch in bright, red explosions. I heaved a sigh, knowing the wind would die down eventually. Everything does. Everything either dies down or burns down.

Lilly and I sang "Happy Birthday" to Gramps before leaving him on the edge of some woods. Birds fluttered down from the dark trees overhead and began pecking at the charred meat.

At last, the wind ceased. The hem of Lilly's dress remained straight, unaffected by any breeze. My hair laid as it should. I filled my lungs with hot, still, night air. Fireworks sounded in the distance, intermingling with Ricky's agonized screams.

He'd be more black and blue than a Hell's Angels bar fight by the time we returned. We listened to exploding firecrackers, those high-pitch Screaming Meemies, those terrible, bursting Roman candles, and whatever other explosives were being fired into the night.

People out there were havin' a good time, it seemed.

Well. That's Independence Day in Holebrim, Texas for you.

THE DRIP

I was eleven when we moved into the townhouse in east Saint Paul. Susan had just turned thirteen. Dad went out to get a haircut a few months prior and never returned. Mom liked to say Dad was too embarrassed by his new hairdo to ever show himself again. It was one of those unfunny jokes she made when her feelings were hurt. So, it was just us three in the old, two-story brownstone house.

It was a sweltering August afternoon. Our street was congested with parked cars. The houses were side-by-side with zero space between; a vast change from the rural setting we'd been accustomed to.

I was reading issue twelve of *Tales From the Crypt*, a spooky comic with stories narrated by a haggard old zombie named The Cryptkeeper, when Susan opened wide the front door, inadvertently scraping my lower back. I'd been sitting on the front stoop.

"Ouch!" I said.

"Oh, sorry!" Her blue eyes beamed with excitement. "Come on! You gotta see this!" She darted back inside. I set aside my comic and went in. The linoleum chessboard entryway squeaked beneath my tennis shoes. Mom sat at the kitchen table, drinking from a highball glass.

She had an assortment of liquor bottles up in the cabinet above the oven. I tried a sip from one of the bottles once. It made my throat burn and my lips pucker like I'd eaten sour candy. I never touched the stuff again. Often, I wished Mom would've done the same.

She smiled, waving lackadaisically as I passed, as if she were in a dream. A beam of sunshine settled upon her gaunt, freckled cheeks. The glass sweated in her hand. The bottle clinked as she poured another. Susan stood on the stairwell, beckoning me upstairs.

"Come on!" she said, tromping up to the second floor. I followed her past my room, past Mom's, to the walk-in closet at the end of the hall. Susan coaxed the overhead bulb into illumination. Barren shelves were coated with grey dust. In the corner was a stack of moving boxes yet un-opened. She went inside, then leaned against the left-side brick wall. I stood at the doorway, one eyebrow raised as high as it could go.

"Great," I said. "You found the closet."

"No, idiot." She laughed. "Don't you hear it? Listen."

I listened, and heard nothing. I raised both eyebrows now, an expression equivalent to: *Have you lost your marbles, Susan?*

She merely nodded toward the wall. I frowned, at last hearing something. It was faint, like a cry in a thunderstorm. I put my ear to the wall.

Drip. Drip. Drip.

Like the ticking of a clock, the drip was dependable and rhythmic. I straightened.

"Something's leaking behind this wall!"

She rolled her eyes. "No, duh."

"We better tell Mom about this," I said, turning away.

"No!" Susan said, grabbing my shoulder. "Don't. She won't care anyway. She doesn't care about anything."

"That's not true," I protested.

"You know what *is* true?" she asked. A secret burned in the sly tilt of her mouth.

"What?" I asked.

"This wall, in fact, is a door."

I scoffed, placing my hands upon it. The bricks were cool beneath my palms. I pushed. Nothing gave.

"You're fooling with me," I said. "It's not a door. It's just a wall with a hollow spot behind it and there's a pipe that's damaged or something."

"Oh yeah?" She pushed me aside, then grunted, using all her force to roll back the clandestine door. I watched her slide the wall to the back of the closet with silent awe. We now stood in front of a gaping black entryway.

Something dripped in the dark. I could hear it clearly, as the droplet of water or whatever it was struck stone.

Drip.

Drip.

Drip.

Susan grabbed my hand, pulling me into the darkness.

"No," I yelled, reeling backward. "It's too dark."

"Don't be a scaredy," she said. "There's light the farther you go in, see? Look where I'm pointing."

The dark hallway stretched onward, like a tube-shaped dungeon. At the very end, a door with a green light creeping out at its bottom.

“What is this place?” I asked.

“I don’t know,” Susan replied, her eyes still beaming with excitement. “Let’s check it out.”

As we walked, the light from the closet behind us grew dim. The hallway walls were constructed of rouge brick, tinged with black slime. The hallway reverberated with our whispers. Mildewed air tickled my nostrils. Cobwebs swayed from high corners. I did not feel a draft.

"Listen, Suz, let's go back. Please?"

"No." She remained confident and poised. She held an elegantly crafted brass key, featuring the emblem of a human skull. It was grinning.

"Whoa!" I said. "What's that?"

"Skeleton key. The door up ahead is locked, but this should open it."

"Where'd you get it?"

"From Mom."

"She just *gave* it to you?"

She shrugged, avoiding my shrewd gaze.

"You stole it," I noted, matter-of-factly.

"She wasn't doing anything with it anyway!"

"Where did you find it? Her room?"

"Of course not," she scolded. "What do you think I am, some kind of snoop?"

"Where then?" I prompted.

"Mom's cabinet above the oven."

"What were you doing looking in there?"

She said nothing, but I had a good idea as to the answer.

Our footsteps echoed down the passageway. The dripping grew closer. The door loomed before us, its ebony wood paint-chipped and flaking. Susan inserted the key into the rust-eaten lock. The lime green glow pulsing beneath the one inch breach at the door's bottom made my flesh crawl.

"Wait." I grabbed her hand. "I've got a bad feeling about this."

"Garrett," she sighed. "What grade will you be in next September?"

"Fifth," I replied, with a swell of pride.

"Well, you're acting like you're in first."

I deflated like a popped balloon. My fear of what lay beyond the door resurfaced, grabbing hold like an iron vice. The possibilities were endless. The green glow led me to suspect an infestation of extra-terrestrial breeding pods. Or a grotesque, slimy demon from a supernatural dimension. I've seen enough movies and comic books to know weird things like that happen.

"Susan? Garrett?" The voice drifted down the dank hall like a tune carried on a breeze. Susan and I spun around to face the entrance, where the closet's yellow light waded in. Mom's silhouette leaned against the wall.

"You kids get out of there!" Her voice was ragged with fear now, echoing off the walls and ceiling. Susan withdrew the skeleton key, stuffing it into her black denim jacket.

"Don't tell her about the key," she whispered. "Promise?"

I blinked. "Okay, I guess."

"Not 'I guess'." She shook my shoulders. "Promise!"

"All right, all right," I said. "I promise."

"GARRETT! SUSAN!"

We ran down the long, dark passageway and into the light of the closet. Mom pulled us into a tight hug, her face a portrait of fear and confusion. My face pressed uncomfortably into her hard ribs.

"I never knew this was here," she said, her words somewhat slurring. "How'd you kids find it?"

"I went looking for some clothes," Susan explained. "Thought they might still be in one of the boxes. Then I heard this dripping behind the wall. I leaned on it just enough that it budged. So I just kept pushing it, until the hallway appeared. Neat, huh?"

"No," Mom replied, shaking her head. "It's . . . freaky. From now on, you two are to stay out of there. Got it?"

I nodded. I didn't want to see what was behind that door anyway.

"But, Mom!" Susan protested.

"No buts," she said, and hiccupped. "There's probably mold spores and all kinds of hazards in there. Go outside guys, all right? It's a sunny day."

Mom pushed the sliding barrier back into place, then clapped her hands of rouge dust. We followed her downstairs, where she fixed herself another drink. Susan went to her room, slamming the door. My comic was waiting for me on the stoop. I tried to read, yet became distracted by the sound of the dripping inside my head.

***

At midnight, I was awoken by the creaking of floorboards outside my room. Tossing aside my Anakin Skywalker blanket, I tip-toed into the hallway. To my right, Mom's door was closed. To my left, the light of the open closet pooled onto the floor.

The now not-so-secret entryway was opened. I gazed down the long, dark tunnel and felt as if I were looking down the barrel of a gun. My body shivered with gooseflesh.

Drip.

Drip.

Drip.

Amidst the drips, footsteps. "Susan?” I called into the dark. “That you?"

My words echoed back. The terror in my voice made me feel like a coward. A deep breath strengthened my resolve, and I entered the passageway. The glimmering green of the door lay ahead. The soles of my feet burned upon the icy cold cobblestone floor. Mildew and dirt flooded my nostrils. It was suddenly difficult to breathe, as if my lungs were coated with the slime of the walls.

I stood before the door. The glowing was brighter, flaring with lime-hued flashes. The steady drip resounded in my ears. My hand settled upon the cold brass knob. It turned freely, unlocked. Had Susan come through with the key? Was she inside the room? Was she in danger?

. . . Was she dead?

Images of terrible green slime-monsters bombarded me. They ate my sister while she screamed, her blood splattering everywhere.

But there was only silence. And the drip.

Getting onto my knees, I peered through the keyhole. The entire room was filled with verdant mist. And yet, passing before my eyes, shadows. Curling and dipping, as if there were multiple people --- or things --- inside the room.

Then, someone standing directly behind the door, its dark frame blocking my vision. My heart pounded. I scuttled backwards like a crab. The door opened.

Susan, shrouded in the swirling green. Something sluiced across the floor behind her. Abruptly pulling the door shut, she turned the skeleton key with a click, then faced me. Darkness circled her eyes. Her face was pale and thin and her blonde hair had turned grey. She looked like Mom.

"Susan?" I asked, my chest rising and falling with panic. I expected her to behave robotically, like some sort of humanoid or alien imitation. Yet she responded with her usual good-natured warmth.

"What are you doing up, dumb-dumb?"

"I heard the dripping," I replied, with a sigh of relief. "What'd you find, Sis? Where's the dripping come from?"

She gazed despondently down at the cobblestone.

"I saw things moving in there." I pointed to the keyhole. “What's in there, Susan? Tell me.”

She shook her head, smiling a sad, knowing smile, as if she knew something I was too young or immature to understand. At last, she said, "*Suffering* is in that room, Garret. Pure, horrible suffering. It's in the air . . . the green stuff. It shows you things. Awful things you don't ever wanna see." Tears spilled down her cheeks.

“Susan?” I asked. “Are you all right?”

She shook her head and walked away. I caught a last glimpse of the pulsing green beneath the door, then followed her back to the closet.

We shut the sliding barrier. Sis returned to her room without further word. I returned to mine and was scarcely able to sleep. I tossed and turned in a night of dull repetition.

Drip. Drip. Drip.

Drip. Drip. Drip.

It made my mind ache. It wasn’t until early morning that I fell asleep, pondering the nature of Susan's words. "Suffering is that room," she'd said. "Pure, horrible suffering."

***

Weeks passed. Susan grew more ill every day, withering into grotesque emaciation. Mom drove her to endless doctors' appointments and hospital overnights. None of it made any difference. Susan's head was jaundiced and shrunken, her skin like parchment stretched taut over bones. Mom was certain it was cancer, although all the tests came back negative.

It was the final day of August, as autumn winds blew against the windowpanes. Susan was dying. Mom and the hospice nurse, an old lady named Gerda, talked in the hallway. Susan lie in her bed, grey hair splayed upon the pillow. She'd become a skeleton.

"I love you, Sis," I said, failing to stave off the tears.

"I love you." Her lips, chapped and withered, mouthed the words more than said them.

"Susan," I said. "You're dying because of what's in that room, aren't you? You have to tell exactly what you saw. If the doctors know what you're dying from, they might be able to save you."

She heaved a sigh. Her fetid breath smelled of the passageway, all moist earth and mildewed brick. Her eyes, glazed and yellowed, were so old that for a moment it seemed impossible this person could be Susan. And yet, gleaming in the back of her eyes, I recognized my sister --- flickering, fading away, her vitality leaking out of her, drop by drop.

"Garret." My name came out in a croak. "Be careful . . . the drip."

This last came out in one syllable: *thedrip.*

Her eyes rolled up into the back of her head, exposing two yellow moons. Her throat clicked. Sporadic breaths escaped her.

"Mom!" I shouted, my heart pounding. "Come quick!"

Mom ran into the room, and seeing, threw herself upon the bed. She grabbed Susan's shoulders and squeezed. She pleaded, "Susan, honey, please, stay with us. Don't go. Not yet. *Please.*"

Susan fell slack-jawed and breathless against Mom's chest. Her eyes remained half-open, like a zombie. Gerda, the nurse, checked for a pulse, then shook her head. Mom looked at me wearily with despair in her eyes, then collapsed into shoulder-hitching sobs. Gerda put her arms around her, murmuring soothing reassurances. My heart was crushed. I could no longer stand the dreadful atmosphere, so I left the room.

I sat down at the kitchen table, crowded with the detritus of empty bottles. My stomach churned. Distinctly, I heard it.

I heard it from all the way upstairs, through the closet, down the dark passageway, behind that damned, ancient door with its green secret smothering its cold body against the wood.

Drip. Drip. Drip.

***

Four days after Susan's funeral, Mom drove me to the new school for my first day of fifth grade. The September sky was grey, reminding me of Susan's hair. I scanned the city streets, people-watching. Men my father's age, dressed in business suits, carrying briefcases, going to work. A woman wearing headphones, walking her dog. We turned onto Cleveland Avenue, where the outcrop of commercial buildings appeared older, much like our house. My eyes widened at the man standing in front of a narrow alleyway, drinking from a bottle concealed by a crinkled, brown paper bag. Our eyes locked briefly, then we'd passed him.

"Mom," I shouted. "Pull over!'

"What? Why?"

"Dad! I just saw Dad!"

"No, you didn't, Garrett." Her eyes focused on the road ahead.

My fists clenched, angered by her no-nonsense tone. How could she be certain I hadn't seen my father? Doesn't a boy know his dad when he sees him? I opened my mouth, about to say as much, then abruptly closed it.

She was crying.

"Mom?"

"I have to tell you something," she sniffled.

"What's wrong?" I asked, gently touching her shoulder.

She heaved a sigh. "Your father isn't with us anymore, honey. He died."

The air seemed to catch in my lungs, as if I'd been kicked in the chest. Her white knuckles gripped the wheel. My tongue clicked dryly.

"How, Mom?" I asked, my voice sounding small.

"He drowned," she replied, wiping her cheeks of mascara. "H-he was out one night. About a week ago. Your Daddy had too much to drink. People pass out sometimes, when they've drank too much. He was on a bridge. He fell over the side, into the river. I'm so sorry, Garret."

I shut my eyes and imagined ice cold water rushing into my father's lungs, the world around him already blackened, blotted out with drunkenness. It then occurred to me my father had died of two drownings: one from the river, and one from the drink.

My world, too, had blackened. A sense of anger and helplessness dampened everything. I thought back to the sunny day we'd first moved into the house. How I'd simply sat on the stoop and read my comic. I yearned, *ached*, for that brief, happy moment again.

Now, it seemed everything good was eroding before me.

Drip by drip.

***

Mom picked me up from school in the evening. We drove in silence. Her breath smelled rancid; a cross between plaque build-up and alcohol. As we turned onto our street, she said, "Garrett . . . I know I haven't been a perfect mom. I want to do better. I really do. Do you think you can forgive me?"

As soon as she pulled in front of the house, I undid my belt, grabbed my backpack, and exited the car. Perhaps it was a heartless thing to do, but at that moment, I had nothing to give. I was alone in the universe, with no friends, no dad, no sister. And my mother seemed unreal as a mannequin, a token symbol of a parent, but not the real thing. If that's what she wanted me to forgive, I couldn't.

I sat on Susan's bed, and read her diary. It was quiet in her room, and a bit creepy. The white wallpaper had yellowed and lifted over the past few weeks, as if it'd absorbed some of Susan's sickness.

Scrawled in the diary were sad poems about Dad. Poems about Mom and her absent-minded drinking. My heart skipped a beat upon reading her last entry, a poem titled, *The Suffering,* featuring lines about *wicked, green tendrils* and a *terrible, dripping death.*

Mom called me into the kitchen for dinner. I pecked at the spaghetti, which had come out of a can. Mom drank from a large glass and stared at the floor. Amidst the silence, the drip began to sound, like the tolling of a hideous bell. *Drip. Drip. Drip.*

I asked Mom if she could hear it too. She looked at me a long time, her eyes drunken and glazed. They frightened me, those eyes. There seemed to be little left behind them.

"I've always heard it," she replied. "Even before we moved into this house. Your father did, too."

***

Within the quiet of my room . . . that dreaded sound of liquid falling and hitting stone. It sounded too close for comfort. Groggily, I lumbered out of bed into the hall.

In front of the open closet, beneath the circumference of the bulb's light, a whiskey bottle lay on its side. Because of the hallway's slanted floorboards, the alcohol tilted toward the bottle's mouth, and dripped. A puddle collected around it.

I picked up the half-empty bottle and set it aside. I went into the closet and looked down the dark passageway. Mom stood before the door. The same eerie, emerald light glowed at the edges and the breach. She unlocked it, then walked inside.

"Mom," I shouted. "Wait!" Running down the long passageway, I feared the worst --- that the green suffering thing behind the door would get her too. Just as it had gotten Susan. The thought of another two weeks of prolonged agony and death ripped open my heart, made me want to writhe on the floor and scream.

My toe caught on a dislodged piece of cobblestone. I fell forward onto my chest. The wind knocked out of me. I wheezed, gulping in nothing, until air flooded my lungs. I got onto my feet. My big toe nail was ripped clean off, revealing a slick, bloody patch of flesh. My foot throbbed with pain, but I had no time to worry about this.

The skeleton key stuck out from the lock. I pocketed it, grabbed the doorknob coated with verdigris, and on the count of three, flung the door open.

I walked into thick green fog. Dense, moist air crawled and slithered over my body, as if I were cloaked in insects and serpents. A few feet further, I turned around and could no longer see the door through the swampy haze. As I breathed, my lungs filled with the stuff, making me nauseous. Something slid over my bare feet. When I looked down, it was gone. Yet it had left behind a trail of slime, like green Jell-O. My feet were wet with it. "Mom?" I cried. "Where are you?!"

A low groan emanated across the room. I followed the sound, until discovering two silhouettes sitting on the ground, their backs against the wall.

"Who-who's there?" I asked.

My mother's voice, soothingly familiar, replied, "Everything's okay, honey. Come on over."

I got down on my haunches, so as not to lose her in the swirling green. Once I was close enough to make out the features of my mother's face, and of the man sitting next to her --- I gasped, clamping a hand over my mouth.

Bile rose in my throat. I vomited onto the grimy floor. The man sitting beside her laughed --- my father's laugh.

He raised a bottle of Budweiser to his corroded lips and drank deeply. His face was a liquefied potpourri of worms, roaches, and tiny, yellow maggots. His eyes were gone. Slick, green seaweed hung from the hollows. Scarce patches of moist, decaying flesh clung to the forehead and cheeks. The rest was ivory bone.

My heart crammed up into my throat. The flesh dripped off his withered face and arms, onto the floor.

"Don't be scared, honey," Mom grinned, her teeth rotten. Slushy molars dribbled down the corner of her lips. "It's just your *Daddy.*"

Her eyes, sunken and pig-like, beamed with cruelty. Worst of all --- the flesh of her face beaded, then dripped off her form like candlewax. Her nose, forehead, cheeks, lips, and eyes drooped, and I screamed.

They laughed as I scrambled to my feet. The atmosphere clung to every inch of my body, even sticking to my insides. My heart, lungs, and intestines were smothered, grasped by the green tendrils of suffering. My insides began to melt. Running my hands alongside the far wall, I followed it until, thank god, I discovered the door.

A frigid hand gripped my ankle. Susan's face grinned up at me, her head shrunken to the size of an apple. The scrunched face was a ball of wrinkles with yellow eyes; wet and crawling with grubs like the underside of a log. "*Thedrip,*" she croaked. "*Thedripthedripthedrip!*"

I shrieked, yanking loose from her grasp. I slammed the door shut behind me and locked it with the key. Limping back to the closet, my foot trailed blood. Their abhorrent laughter hadn't ceased. Nor had the dripping.

I rolled shut the secret door, then ran downstairs and called 911. I shuddered so hard, was so out of breath, the receptionist could barely understand what I was saying.

***

Having lost my family, I was bounced between foster homes until old enough to live independently. I'm a grown man now, with an affectionate wife and a beautiful, young daughter. Johanna has deep, brown eyes, just like her mother, Sarah. We live in a modest house in the country, and we are happy.

Some nights, when the wife and I are relaxing on the couch, reading a bedtime story to our sweet Johanna, I feel something stir within my chest.

It's the green tendrils, curling around my heart; like seaweed at the bottom of a river, seeking to consume the things that have fallen.

But I have not fallen. And I never intend to. Neither shall I ever fall prey to the bottle. I want to be there for Johanna, and for Sarah, as long as I live.

Sometimes, late at night, when my girls are fast asleep, I hear that dreadful clockwork *drip-drip-drip*. I get out of bed and stand in my daughter's doorway, gazing upon her sleeping, moon-shadowed face, knowing in my heart that I would never want be without her or her mother. I am overcome with a sense of strength and goodness.

And the green tendrils of suffering unfurl; shrinking, fading, dripping . . . away.

GODLY BUSINESS

The body of God fell out of an azure sky on a humid June morning. One hundred and thirty acres of golden Nebraskan wheat contained just enough space for the body. God's head was as big as the nearby two-story farmhouse. A cotton-white beard, now matted with blood, led from the Almighty's chin to the front porch.

Eddie Rednick, fifty-eight-year-old businessman and professional penny-pincher, was jarred awake by the after-tremors. He ambled out of bed and onto the porch. His frown lines deepened. Like a royal carpet, the flowing white beard led him down the steps, around the house and into the field. He wiped sleep from his eyes with the back of his hands and looked again.

A giant occupied his acreage. A shimmery white tunic, now stained Moscato red, clung to the body. Rednick approached the head, around which an ankle-high pool of gore had collected. He could not see the face. It was smashed into the field. Crimson-splattered wheat stirred in the breeze. A tangy odor of copper wafted under Rednick's pock-marked nose. In one direction, long white arms snaked through the wheat. In the other, long, hairy legs and a thick torso claimed the land.

Rednick scratched his balding head and stood before the body of God, pondering what the hell he was looking at.

And what the hell to do about it.

***

There was something in the blood. A magical, life-giving property of some kind. Eddie discovered this by inadvertently slipping in the blood-pool around God's enormous head. He’d landed hard on his shoulder, half of his face submerging into the pool. He'd lifted up his head, mouth full of blood. The initial revulsion fizzled away, replaced by a pleasant tingling upon his tongue and the roof of his mouth. The blood tasted sweetly delicious. Not salty like he'd expected.

Cupping his palms, he scooped the blood and drank with reverence, as if he were sipping the waters of the Rubicon. Power and vitality coursed through his veins. The decades-old ache in his back was gone. Eddie Rednick, a relatively old man, leapt to his feet. Blood dripped down his face and body. He licked his lips, his eyes wide, dilated with inspiration.

He understood everything. He understood who the dead giant was. He understood the power of His Blood and Flesh. Most of all, he understood he was damned fortunate. A goldmine had landed on his property. *Now,* he thought, *good ol' Rednick is going to reap the riches! God, after all, is a rare commodity.*

Eddie spent all morning and afternoon cleaning old mason jars and filling them with Holy Blood. He made a run into town, buying out *Alma's Antiques'* stock of jars, then filled those too.

Around six that evening, he wiped sweat from his forehead and propped his feet upon the kitchen table. Hundreds of blood-filled mason jars occupied the counters and linoleum floor. He made a phone call to town councilman, Simon Kohl, securing his selling booth for Jessup Township's Annual Farmer's Market.

Rednick celebrated with a jar he'd stuck in his refrigerator. Sipping cold, refreshing blood, he smacked his stained lips in delight. Then his eyes enlarged and his mouth fell open. A small globe, coated with shimmering oceans and green continents, formed upon the palms of his hands. The planet rotated slowly. If he peered closely, he could see tiny people walking about, driving cars, flying airplanes, setting off bombs, fucking and fighting each other at a furious clip.

Rednick closed his eyes. When he opened them, the planet was gone from his hands, its presence no more than a vague sensation in the back of his mind, like a hazy dream upon awakening.

He grinned. The blood contained more magical properties than he'd realized. Once people understood what it could do, it was only a matter of time before the money rolled in. He licked the blood from his lips.

***

Eddie Rednick's Special, Life-Giving Concentrate circled each tin lid in a black, inky scrawl. *The Blood of God* written at the center. On the back of each jar was a *Not FDA approved, but Holy Ordained!* sticker.

Operating out of the back of his Chevrolet pick-up, Eddie managed to sell two hundred and thirteen jars, each at the ultra-moderate price of $15.99. Residents of Jessup, thinking the 'blood of God' label a gimmick and the stuff was probably a juice of some kind, drank from the sample-sized serving cups . . . then grinned ecstatic, insisting they purchase a jar. Rednick happily obliged. By day's end, he'd earned enough cash to drive into the nearby city and buy himself a top-of-the-line storage freezer.

As a businessman, he recognized opportunity when he saw it. Blood alone would not be the only commodity he capitalized. *As ol' Pastor Dan says during Sunday Communion,* Rednick thought, watching two delivery men haul his recent purchase into his house, *drink of my Blood, and eat of my Flesh.*

***

A moonlit prairie night. God's carcass was pale as the underbelly of a fish. Bats flittered across the stars. Crickets chirruped. The chainsaw's harsh roar soon drowned them out. Wearing a butcher's apron, Eddie positioned the saw over the Almighty's right side. The chain spun, ripping and tearing away flesh to reveal the rare, precious meat beneath.

"Dee-vine rib!" Eddie chuckled as the saw sputtered into silence. He hauled two buckets of bloody meat into the house to clean, package, and freeze. Yet he'd hardly made a dent in God's enormous body. He'd need some assistance slicing up the rest. An extra storage freezer, too. Dunking his hand into a bucket, he fished out a chunk of raw flesh and shoved it into his mouth.

He chewed vigorously, swallowed, then gasped at the beautiful colors suddenly gleaming upon his palms. The planet formed once again; a gorgeous world brimming with life. The Blood had made him aware of the planet's presence. But the Flesh now gave him the power to control the fate of every person, every creature, every aspect about the planet. Eddie didn't know how he knew this to be so, only that he did.

Centering his attention upon one of the oceans, Eddie willed into existence a tremendous tsunami. The cyclone of wind and water moved

West, decimating dozens of cities upon one of the larger continents, murdering hundreds of thousands of people.

Eddie spent the rest of the night messing around with the planet. He felt like a child again, sitting atop his favorite anthill to scorch, stomp, and drown the ants. Cocking his ear close to the living sphere, he smiled so big his dentures threatened to pop out. Way down on what remained of the planet's land mass, he heard thousands of people . . . screaming.

"Now this," he told the empty room. "This is *money!*"

***

Eddie Rednick wasn't just a man anymore, but a brand.

Hiring ads in Jessup's bi-weekly newspaper were answered within a week. Ten young men, most of them fresh out of high school, came down to Eddie's for a job. Eddie obliged them, begrudgingly paying minimum wage. Nine dollars an hour was far too high in Eddies' estimate.

"But it's the law," the kids insisted.

"Damn unions," Eddie muttered, supervising his employees as they stripped God's flesh with an assortment of chainsaws, butcher's knives, and axes.

It was nearly July. Weather was hot. The body was beginning to smell. A rancid stench of decay cloyed to the humid air. Occasionally, one of the young workers would step away from the body, bend at the waist and puke. Eddie shaded his eyes from the sun, frowning as they worked at the body, grunting and cursing like a bunch of ungrateful slaves.

Over the next few days, buckets, wagons and wheelbarrows of God's flesh were taken away, cleaned, packaged, and shipped to local supermarkets. As were thousands of jars of blood.

Eddie watched his slavish crew of Gen Z's closely. If he didn't, they'd slack off. The first day they were hired, several took pictures with their smartphones. Instagram selfies; posing with bloody knifes in their hands, the giant body in the background.

But it was their second week now. Instagram was a thing of the past. They'd all had a complimentary taste of the Blood and Flesh. Which meant each had their own, precious planet. One they could manifest into their hands with a little will and imagination.

Jared or Jeremy --- whatever the kid's name was--- stopped work to do just that. Butcher's knife resting atop the back of God's knee, the blonde-haired boy laughed, spinning his planet five hundred times faster than its normal orbit speed. Eddie could hear the tiny screams from fifty yards away, where he stood in the shade.

"Hey YOU," Eddie shouted.

The kid looked up. Frowned.

"Yeah, you! Put that away. I ain't payin' ya to play God, son. I'm payin' ya to work."

The young man rolled his eyes, then closed them, willing the planet back into his imagination. He picked up his axe and got back to hacking.

"That's better, twerp," Eddie muttered, then went into the house to catch up on FOX News. Several anchors were singing his praises.

***

Bernard Rednick, Eddie's father, had been a businessman. All Eddie's life, Bernard had encouraged him to embrace the ultra-American values of entrepreneurship and unfettered capitalism. Bernard had made his life in the petroleum business. He was able to retire early. Yet the retirement was short-lived. Plagued by life-long obesity and diabetes, Bernard died of a heart attack. Aged forty-six.

Eddie had expected to inherit his father's millions. Alas, he did not. In Bernard's will, it was stipulated his son would embrace hard work and do it all on his own. Just as his father had.

Eddie attempted to operate several businesses throughout the years. Each failed miserably. A two-year degree in business management hadn't helped in the least. Money was never made, and if by some stroke of luck it was, it was lost just as quickly.

But now, he thought, *now it's different. I'm finally getting my lucky break. I'm a successful businessman now, by God! A holy man too. God's Blood and Flesh are mine. And at modest prices, I'm sharing Him with the world.*

Tears welled in his eyes. He only wished his old man could be here to see him now. He longed to hear his father's gruff voice telling him how proud he was. Something Eddie never got to hear.

Blinking away tears, he set his glass of blood upon the living room coffee table. He closed his eyes, willing the planet into his hands. He focused on the continent replicated after America, then centered in on Boston, Massachusetts, then 122nd Street where his childhood home had been. Peering into his father's bedroom window, he discovered Bernard sitting at the end of his bed, tying his red power tie.

Eddie whispered his father's name.

Bernard frowned, looked all about the bedroom. "Martha honey? That you?"

"No! It's me, Dad."

Bernard stood, loose tie hanging from his collar. "Edward?" He looked in the closet, then under the bed. "Where are you, kiddo? What the hell you doing in here?"

Eddie laughed boomingly. His father jumped, knocking over the bedside lamp. Eddie ceased laughing. He'd forgotten how large and, consequently, how loud he was.

"Sorry, Father. Didn't mean to startle you. Just wanted to let you know I'm running a business now. A very successful one at that. I'm not as successful as you yet, but soon enough, I will be."

"H-how are you doing this?" Bernard asked, back flat against the wall, sweaty hands pressing upon the floral-print wallpaper. "Where are you? Give up the joke."

"I'm above you, Father," Eddie replied in a whisper. "In heaven, I'd guess you'd say. You see, I'm selling the Flesh and Blood of God up here. I've made myself in his Divine Image. Better yet, I've made myself a businessman! Aren't you proud of me, Father?"

Sweat beaded Bernard's face. He shook his head, mumbled he was going crazy. Looney. Buggy. Hearing voices.

"Daddy?" Eddie's voice suddenly broke, choking back tears. "Just . . . tell me you're proud of me. Won't you? You've never said it, you know. No matter how hard I've tried to please you, both as a child, and as a man. So, tell me. I need to hear it, Daddy. Please."

Eddie waited for reply.

At last, Bernard scowled. "Whoever you are, you're not my son. You're a monster. A demon. Now get the hell out of my room! Get out of my head! I hate you! Hate, hate, hate!"

Bernard picked up the bedside lamp and threw it across the room. The bulb shattered upon the wall. The shade cracked. Eddie's heart palpitated. Tears dripped from his eyes, fell into the planet's atmosphere, and struck the roof of Bernard's house. In that instant, Bernard was crushed beneath fallen timber. Nails. Chimney bricks.

Eddie's tears dripped from his chin in a flood. They splashed down, drowning Boston and obliterating the remains of his father's house. Then Eddie willed the planet back into his head. Even with all his power, will and control, he could not change his old man's heart.

Eddie snatched a bottle of Jack Daniels from the mini bar across the room, drinking until unconscious.

***

ONE YEAR LATER

Behind the three-story Rednick Mansion, Eddie led a guided tour of a hundred people around his field. First, he showed them God's enormous, hollowed out skull. Parents snapped pictures of their young children hunkered within the eye sockets. Horseflies buzzed thick around the carcass. Few seemed to mind.

Eddie guided them from the cranium to the neck vertebrae, down to the shoulders, arms, hands, torso, legs, feet. Bringing them back 'round to the skull, the tour was complete. The children clamored for a second tour. Their parents informed them it was too expensive, encouraging them to play with their planets instead.

People marveled over the remains, much like they did over the fossils of extinct dinosaurs at the Museum of Natural History. Eddie laughed at their foolishness and pocketed the cash. What was a pile of bones to him?

Money, of course. Nothing more.

He was a businessman, and blood and flesh alone would not satiate his holy, entrepreneurial spirit. Eddie figured the word God was merely a euphemism for Capital. He fumbled with the golden crucifix around his neck, trying his best not to pick his nose with it in front of the crowd.

No more Blood. No more Flesh. But there were bones.

Bones and endless money.

God's skeleton, one might aptly say, was Eddie Rednick's church.

And by the Will of the Almighty Dollar, the congregations flocked.

Eddie was happy to evangelize. All the better without the Bible. Hundred-dollar bills were scripture enough. After all, *In God We Trust* was printed on each and every one of them.

With God's shimmery, blood stained tunic sold to a European theological museum for billions of dollars, and His cotton-white beard snipped and sold by the baggie, there seemed to be no end to this holy profitable exploitation.

Yessir, Eddie Rednick smiled, *from now on, life is going to be nothing but sweet, sweet money.*

***

FIVE HUNDRED AND THIRTY-THREE YEARS LATER

The years had been anything but sweet. When Eddie Rednick turned seventy, yet still appeared fifty-seven in the mirror, he'd been elated. The Blood and Flesh of God had preserved his soul for eternity. He was immortal. No death for Rednick. Nor for the millions who'd consumed even a parcel of God's bounty. What could be better?

Alas. Immortality was not all it was cracked up to be. Eddie sat upon the scorched Earth, over five hundred years old, yet still fifty-seven. Black clouds of smoke covered the sky. The sun rarely peaked through them. For the last seventy years, he'd not seen another living soul . .

. except those tiny man-ants upon his planet, of course. They hardly counted.

He spent his time creating people, animals, cities, beautiful utopias. Then destroying them. He did it for the same reason children used to construct elaborate sandcastles, then destroy them. Because it was entertaining. At the very least, it was something to do.

World War Four had destroyed the world completely. Everything was charcoal. Ash. Noxious smoke. Scattered remains. Worse yet, there was nothing to do. Eddie ached for death. His soul was parched. He now knew with dreadful certainty why God had fallen out of the sky that warm June morning in the first place. For God had grown bored and loathsome with His own immortality. He'd therefore killed Himself in the only way feasible for an immortal being --- sacrifice himself to the world He had created.

The nuclear bombs had not affected the immortals --- the men, women and children who'd long ago consumed the Flesh and Blood. The radiation had not mutilated their flesh, ravaged their internal organs, nor suffocated them like all the others --- the mortals. The fortunates.

The only way out was to will the planets out of their minds and into their hands, then will themselves into *that* world. They'd fall through a smoke-free blue sky before crashing to their death into the land or the sea.

Eddie held back from doing this. He didn't know why. Despite his hatred of immortality, perhaps he was too cowardly a man, too significant an ego, to embrace death.

Yet as the blackness swarmed upon the Earth, as green, radioactive winds flurried from place to place in hot, violent airstreams, Eddie found himself willing his mind and body into the tranquil blue-green planet, the miniature Earth within his hands. He squeezed his eyes shut, focusing, until . . . cool, soothing wind rippled his tattered clothes.

He managed to open his eyes against the pressure, squinting at the beautiful planet beneath. Eddie smiled. It was not as scary as he'd thought it'd be. The roar of the wind sounded in his ears. The green continent below grew very close, then . . .

***

Tremors ran through the city. Buildings, houses and streets became rubble. Upon the splintered asphalt, toppled electric poles and decimated structures, lay the body of a giant.

Police, firefighters, and citizens surrounded it. Blood flowed out of the body, pouring ankle-deep through the streets, flooding the gutters, drowning the people still trapped beneath the rubble.

Covered with debris and gore, the people exchanged flabbergasted expressions. They approached the body of Eddie Rednick, of God. In one unanimous moment of realization, everyone smiled.

After endless generations of bloodshed, of worldwide floods, fires, volcanic eruptions, cataclysmic earthquakes, and the ancient, perpetual voice of a deranged Man in the Sky bombarding their ears about money, money, money . . . They understood, at long last, they were free.

Free of the Thing Called Eddie Rednick, Businessman.

Free of the Great Terror in the Sky.

Free!

BOX OF CHOCOLATES

The white tile floor gleamed beneath fluorescent lights. It hurt his eyes. *Stop looking at the floor then, dummy*, he told himself. His gaze settled upon the shelves. He pushed the grocery cart down the aisle, the front wheels sticking, always drifting to the right. He cursed under his breath.

Angela, his girlfriend of three years, had packed up her things and left. Now he was on his own. Depressed. Vulnerable. He paused before the hard-shell box of Whitman's assorted chocolates. It seemed to call out to him from its place upon the shelf. Its pallid yellow cover reminded him of daisies. The kind Angela had planted in the flowerpots she'd arranged on his front porch.

Jeremy cared little about flowers. Those daisies, if Angela didn't take them like she'd taken everything else, would surely wilt, grow brittle-brown, then die.

That is how his heart felt; a flower, once blooming with life, now shriveled into the husk of its former self. He put the Whitman's box inside the cart.

***

Angela's mother, a short, scrawny old woman with thick spectacles, opened the door.

"She wants nothing to do with you," she said, blue eyes piercing. "Don't you realize that?"

Jeremy nodded. "Yes, Estelle. I realize that, but--"

"Then go away."

"I just wanted to talk to--"

"*No.*" Her lips were tucked into a thin line.

He sighed. "There's some things she left at my house. I'm wondering if she wants them back."

"What things?" she snapped. "Angela said she'd already packed everything."

Jeremy struggled for a reply. Angela, in fact, had packed everything. He looked down at the yellow Whitman's box in his hands. A lightbulb went on. "Her flowers!" he shouted, flinching at the volume of his own voice. Estelle's eyes roved over him, as if he were fit for the nut-ward. "I mean," Jeremy explained. "The daisies. She forgot them."

"Keep them," Estelle said. "Can't you see we have enough flowers around here?"

Gardenias, purple tulips and red roses swayed in a breeze beside the front stoop. It was a grey, chilly evening.

“Well, if you're sure she doesn't wanna talk,” he said, “can you at least give her this?"

She snatched the box out of his hands. The door slammed in his face.

Estelle, you old hag, he thought, returning to his Ford pick-up parked in front of the mailbox. It began to rain. Cool droplets splashed the back of his neck. He shivered.

***

"Life is like a box of chocolates," said Forrest Gump in his signature drawl. "You never know what you're gonna get."

Angela's favorite movie played on AMC. Jeremy sat on the couch, downing the night's seventh bottle of Miller. He thought of the Whitman's sampler box Estelle has rudely snatched from him. Then he thought of Angela: her wavy brown hair and emerald eyes. His heart ached like the arthritic bones of an old man during a long week of rain.

He wiped his wet cheeks, popped another cold one, and ambled onto his front porch. Crickets chirruped in the night. The daisies were no more than decrepit weeds, limply rooted within boxes of arid dirt. As the beer bathed his tongue, running down his throat like a cool stream, he regretted his vice.

The drinking was why Angela had left.

The drinking was why the daisies had died.

The drinking was why he was alone on a Saturday night with nothing but the crickets.

Rheee Rheee.

He stepped out into the night, bottle sweating in his hand. Lush, wet grass slicked the soles of his bare feet. He may've been too drunk to drive, but he could still walk to Estelle's house. He'd knock on the door and beg Angela to take him back. A voice in the back of his mind told him he was being a fool, and that he ought to go have a nap on the couch instead.

He ignored that voice.

***

Even with his senses blunted with intoxication, Jeremy knew something was wrong. Estelle's flowers had wilted, drooping sadly toward the ground. The front door stood three inches ajar. The darkness inside cast a shadow across the porch's moonlit floorboards. He set down the beer and pushed open the creaking door.

"Angela?" He swayed down the entrance hall, wet feet slapping linoleum. "Estelle? Anyone home?"

His pulse quickened. Fear. Trepidation. Why had he come here? It was the middle of the night. If Estelle called the cops, things would not look good for him . . . but liquid courage trumped his fear. He wandered into the empty living room. A cold cup of tea sat on a side table next to the couch.

A layer of sweat collected over his brow. He wiped it away. Fear began to sober him. His senses seemed flooded with strange information. What if thieves had broken in, stealing valuable items and killing Angela and her mother in the process?

. . . Yet everything appeared intact. Aside from the door, no signs of disturbance. The dying plants in Estelle's garden had been the only deviation from the norm.

He entered the kitchen. Moonlight streamed through the window over the sink, outlining two silhouettes sitting across from each other at the table. Jeremy's heart crammed up into his throat. Sweat began to eek from his armpits and drip down the bridge of his nose.

"A-Angela, honey?" he asked. "Estelle?"

The shadows at the table remained statuesque.

He flicked on the wall switch, flooding the kitchen with light. He rubbed his eyes, until his vision focused and cleared. Sitting at the table, two human-sized replicas of Angela and Estelle. Not a wrinkle, nor beauty mark, nor hair was out of place on either. The single glaring difference between the women and their replicas was the color. The replicas were smooth, gleaming, uniform brown. Upon the center of the table, the emptied Whitman's chocolates box. Crinkled up wrappers and emptied plastic trays lay beside it.

Jeremy circled the table, studying the figures. Angela's eyes were wide as coffee mugs. Estelle's mouth was tucked into a downward fold; an expression more so of sadness than of fright.

On a whim, he put his nose to Angela's hair. A sweet scent bombarded in his nostrils and his brain said . . . *chocolate?* He sniffed again. Yes, Angela’s replica was composed of chocolate. Estelle's too.

Jeremy sat in the chair between them, riddled with questions. Had Angela and Estelle created these chocolate replicas? If so, for what reason? And where the hell were they, anyway?

He called out their names again, then slumped in his chair, hoping they’d arrive soon.

An hour passed. His stomach rumbled. He eyed the inside of the chocolate box. Every chocolate was gone. Not a single toffee, messenger boy, nor chocolate coated almond remained. His hungry eyes gazed up at Estelle's face.

The impulse circuits of his brain betrayed him. He reached over and yanked Estelle's head off the neck. White, coconut stuffing flowed out of the stub. He devoured the head.

It was the sweetest, most delicious thing he'd ever eaten. His lips were covered with chocolate, and he cared not. Yet his stomach remained growling. He'd not been satiated. He considered Angela.

She would be angry with him once she returned, discovering he'd consumed her replica. Then again, she wasn't his girlfriend anymore, so what did he have to lose? He'd already lost everything. Jeremy found himself taking a knife out of the silverware drawer and cutting into the back of Angela's head.

A thick, red syrup flowed out of the cranium, over the shoulders and down the back of the chair. He set aside the knife, put his lips to the hole, and sucked out every last drop of cherry cordial until the head was no more than a hollow shell.

He ate the shell too.

Holding his bloated belly, he groaned and crumpled into the chair. On his left, a headless chocolate Estelle with white coconut chunks dripping down the stub neck. On his right, a headless Angela with red cherry dripping down her milk chocolate bosom. Out of some strange, perverted instinct, he'd nibbled off her right breast. Cherry syrup continually leaked out the gaping hole, pooling onto the floor.

Jeremy would answer for it later. For now, his eyes closed, and the chocolate hang-over consumed him.

***

A week passed. Jeremy had been correct in his assumption that Angela and Estelle would be angry. He shared the kitchen table with them, their heads gone and their brown shoulders dipped, melting in the sunshine pouring through the window.

The air conditioning had shut off, along with the lights. Probably due to bills going unpaid, Jeremy figured. The women's voices screamed inside his head, where thick, chewy peanut-clusters grew.

Angela hollered at him for eating her head and sucking out the blood. Estelle called him all sorts of names. *That's fine,* he thought. *Let them call me an impulsive bastard. Pretty soon they won't be able to say anything at all. None of us will.*

The sun climbed to its peak in the sky, chimed by the noon bell. A thermometer suction cupped to the window revealed the hottest temperature of the spring, so far. Jeremy felt himself dripping onto the table. His head caved inward, peanut clusters crumbling to the floor.

Angela and Estelle's bodies were soon unrecognizable. Estelle quit screaming inside his mind, turning blessedly silent. Meanwhile, Angela's voice had grown faint.

"Why did you do this to us?" she asked.

"Why did you leave me?" he countered. The back and forth telepathy between their chocolate minds had become almost normal by now.

"Because," Angela replied. "You could never control yourself. A woman likes a man who can make his own decisions. Direct his own life. But you can't even do that."

"Maybe you're right," he admitted, his voice growing weaker. He could feel his consciousness dissolving at equal pace with his body. "But at least I loved you with all my heart. That's more than you can say, Angela. You never loved me. You just pretended to."

"I *did* love you, you idiot," she replied. "I loved you like the daisies I planted for you. But you know, Jeremy, flowers are mature in their love. They respond to rain and sunshine and kind words. You never responded to anything. You were always too drunk. So, I left. Can you blame me?"

Jeremy thought a long time, sunshine curdling his form into a puddle.

"No," he replied. "I can't blame you."

***

The doorbell rang.

"Angela!" Jeremy said, his head and neck now entirely melted. "Someone's here!"

Again, the doorbell. "Angela, did you hear what I said?"

Silence. She'd left him. Again.

The front door creaked open. A little girl in a Girl Scout's uniform wandered into the kitchen. Her eyes widened at the deformed chocolate bodies dripping onto the floor. The sweet scent of chocolate cloyed to the inside of her nostrils.

She walked over to the table, setting down her cardboard box full of Girl Scout cookies and vibrantly colored pamphlets. Jeremy noticed something in the child's blue eyes which reminded him of himself. Without a mouth, Jeremy smiled.

The girl reached out with one scooped hand, removing what remained of Jeremy's heart. The chocolate was sticky on her little hands.

She ate until contented.

THE TYPEWRITER

"Honey, I'm home!" Kendra called. "Look what I picked up for you."

She grunted, clunking the thing down on Andrew's desk. It weighed damn near forty pounds.

"Would you look at that!" he said. "That's a beaut, honey. Where'd you find it?"

"You know that factory you worked at when we first met? Not the one where you assembled motors, but the one with the cables?"

"Ugh," he grumbled. "Don't remind me."

"It's not a factory anymore. They turned the place into a vintage store. Velma's Vintage, it's called. And lo and behold, this was sitting in the corner, practically calling out for me to buy it for you."

Andrew got up from his chair and planted a wet kiss on her lips.

"You're such a sweetie," he said.

"I know," she winked. "I knew you'd love it, 'cause of how old school you are and stuff. The sweet old lady, Velma, said her husband even put a new ribbon in it."

"Very nice."

"Well, what are you waiting for? Go ahead, give it a try!"

"Alright," he said and sat back down.

He scooted the hefty 1941 Royal typewriter in front of him. It scratched lines into the desk, but he didn't care. The desk was nearly as old as the typewriter. He grabbed a piece of Georgia-Pacific paper and rolled it into the paper bale. He began pecking at the keys, feeling an immediate high at the obnoxious clicks and clatters I made.

"Hey, this thing types pretty smooth!" he said. "I'm surprised. Most old typewriters need a good blasting out with a can of penetrating oil to type anything resembling English."

"What did you write?" she asked, peering over his shoulder.

"Here," he said, rolling his chair out of the desk cubby so she could see.

`I have the most wonderful girlfriend ever!`

"Aww, Andrew!" she said. "You're such a kiss ass."

She gave him a peck on the corner of his lips.

"Okay. I've made the boyfriend happy. Now I'm off to hang with Liz for the evening. Do a bit of shopping *for me.*"

"Sure thing, hon. I've only got a few paragraphs left on the column and then I think I'm hanging it up. Put in three hours today. Normally my brain's fried after two."

"That's great, babe. Be back around two or three."

"Kay. See ya in a while. Hey, hon?"

"Yeah?" she asked, turning from the open door.

"Thanks for the typewriter," he said. "It was very thoughtful of you."

"You're welcome," she said, giving a cute shrug. "Love, love, love!"

"Love, love, love," he repeated, and scooted the typewriter aside to finish the article he was writing on the Mac.

***

Andrew wrestled the old push-mower out from under the porch. For a second he had thought the thing would burn up, like a vampire being dragged from its coffin out into sunlight. A strange thought for such a nice day.

The upside to living in a trailer park, he supposed, was that there wasn't a lot of grass to cut. Just one wide, green swatch next to the little sidewalk leading up to the porch. All the same, he was glad to be outside. The hot July sun felt good on his face and shoulders.

An open can of Budweiser sat up in the only tree on their property, a lonely red maple. He had stuck the can in the crook where the first thick branch separated from its trunk. He brought it down and took a swig, then set it back in its designated spot. He jerked back the pull-string and the rusty mower rumbled to life.

He was two-thirds the way down the swatch of grass when he noticed Henry Delane sitting on the front porch of his double-wide, sipping his evening glass of Jameson. He looked pretty philosophical sitting there in the golden light, tranquil, with his trim white beard scuffing the edges of the glass. Henry raised a hand in acknowledgment, then beckoned Andrew to come have a drink with him.

Andrew nodded, pointing down at the mower, as if to say, *maybe I'll take you up on that, right after I've got my five minutes of tough, manly labor over with.* Henry smiled and raised his glass. Then he cocked his head slightly. Andrew followed his gaze.

An old man walking toward him, his face pale and solemn. Andrew released the safety lever, allowing the engine to sputter to a stop. A cascade of sounds far more lovely than the old mower returned to the summer air. The twittering birds. The bees buzzing in Henry's garden. The children playing down the street.

He was a tall, slim man in a frail frame. Pale blue eyes shone through small, round spectacles.

"You Andrew?" the old man asked.

"That's me. How can I help ya?"

"Name's Jim Nicholby," he said, sticking out one trembling, veiny hand.

Andrew shook it.

"And how you can help me," Jim said, "is by being open to negotiating."

"Alright," Andrew said, expecting some lousy sales pitch.

"That damned thing my wife sold your girl. It's no good," he said, shaking his head. "No good at all."

"I'm not sure what you're talking about, Sir."

"That god damned typewriter, son. My wife Velma sold it to *your* wife this morning."

Andrew felt like face-palming. The typewriter. Of course. *Duh.*

"Oh, right," Andrew laughed.

"I'm afraid I'm going to need that typewriter back."

"Why?"

"Velma must've got bored Friday night and decided to rummage through our crawlspace. She found my typewriter, dragged it out of there, slapped a price sticker on it and set it on the sales floor."

Jim slowly shook his head. "I never intended to sell it. Your wife payed fifteen dollars for it. I'd be glad to buy it back for double the amount."

He didn't mind that Jim kept referring to Kendra as his wife. After all, what did it matter?

"That's gracious of you," Andrew said.

"Not at all son, you just hand my baby over and that thirty bucks is yours."

Kendra's yellow Volkswagen pulled into the drive, parking directly behind Andrew's rusty Cavalier.

She climbed out of the car with an armful of groceries. Whenever Kendra told Andrew she was going shopping, usually she only came back with food. It saddened him. He wanted her to treat herself once in a while. The closest she ever came was window-shopping with Elizabeth, her best pal since high school. And, of course, purchasing ol' Jim's typewriter that morning.

"Hey, babe," Andrew said. "Have you met Jim?"

She smiled faintly, setting sunglasses on top of her blonde hair.

"I don't believe I have," she said. "I saw you at Velma's Vintage this morning, didn't I?"

"Yes, ma'am," Jim replied. "Name's Jim Nicholby. Velma's husband."

"Nice to meet you. I think your wife is *such* a doll."

"Can't disagree there," he smiled. "It's just that she makes mistakes, that's all."

"What do you mean?"

Andrew interjected. "Velma sold you Jim's typewriter without knowing he didn't want to sell it. He's kindly offered us a full refund, plus fifteen dollars more if we give it back to him."

Kendra frowned and paused to think for a moment, then shook her head.

"No, I . . . I don't think that's right. It says 'all sales are final' on your store window. That goes both ways, for the customer *and* the seller."

"Now, Kendra," Andrew laughed. "I think Jim's offer is reasonable, don't you?"

"No, not really," she shrugged. "I bought the typewriter because you've been wanting one since we first met. You like it don't you?"

He felt trapped. Of course he liked the typewriter. He really *had* wanted one since before they'd first met. One of the best memories he had as a child was standing on top of a milk crate to type stories on his father's typewriter. It inspired him to pursue a writing career in the first place. Yet he didn't like the typewriter enough to haggle with an eighty-year-old man.

"Yes," Andrew admitted. "I like it."

"Well then, it's settled," she said. "Jim, I'm sorry but we're gonna keep it."

Jim looked down wearily, then perked his head back up as if he'd gotten a bright idea.

"I'll buy it back for a hundred dollars!"

She shook her head, "No. Velma told me it was just sitting in your crawlspace, collecting cobwebs. She said you must've put a ribbon in it recently, since the ink was fresh. But she'd never seen you type on it even once."

"How does two-hundred dollars sound?" he said.

"Sorry. All sales are final. Just as your store policy says."

"Come on now, babe," Andrew said. "Maybe that typewriter is sentimental to him. A part of his family history, maybe?"

"Yes," Jim said, nodding eagerly. "That typewriter belonged to my mother, who used it for her job as an accountant for General Electric. That was way before your time, of course."

Kendra looked at Jim, then gazed up into Andrew's eyes.

"The old man's lying," she whispered. "Velma said he'd found that old typewriter in a *dumpster* five years ago. It can't be that important to him. It's yours now. We're keeping it. Okay?"

She turned to Jim.

"I'm sorry to disappoint you Mr. Nicholby," she said. "Now if you boys will excuse me, I have some groceries to put away."

She climbed the steps to the front porch and entered the trailer, leaving Jim and Andrew standing awkwardly on the grassy strip.

"You've got one strong willed woman, son," Jim frowned. "It's your typewriter, isn't it? Not hers. What do *you* think?"

Andrew wiped the sweat off his forehead, squinting in the sun.

"With all due respect," he said. "I think you're just bummed your wife sold something you'd forgotten you had in the first place."

Jim shook his head. "No. That's not it at all."

"Listen, Kendra's right. We purchased the typewriter, fair and square. Sorry to disappoint."

The old man's hands balled into tight, veiny fists. His jaw clenched.

"You'll be sorry for this," he gritted through his teeth.

Jim reached into his back pocket and grabbed his wallet, pecking out a business card.

"If you change your mind . . ." he said, handing him the card, ". . . not that you'll be able to change your mind by the time that . . . that evil fucking *thing* has gotten to you, give me a call. I'll take it back."

Jim huffed off back across the road and climbed into the truck. He slammed the door and sped off, tires screeching.

Andrew stood there, one hand leaning on the push-mower and the other holding Jim's card. He had the sensation of being watched. He gazed over to his right at Henry Delane, still sitting on his porch, sipping the glass of whiskey. Henry lifted his glass and smiled.

***

Andrew radically changed his writing schedule, simultaneously increasing his productivity and unnerving Kendra. He switched from writing two hours in the morning to writing after dinner, right around 7 p.m., punching the keys like a madman until two in the morning. He'd pass out after a mind-boggling seven hours of writing, then get up just before noon with the hot sun bursting through the blinds. Since he made his living from the comforts of home, he figured he had a right to change his work habits if it meant more money to pay the bills.

Kendra had always known Andrew as an early bird, and to see him transform so quickly into a night owl, typing feverishly away into the late hours, alarmed her. His typing kept her awake nights. The typewriter made a continual click-clack noise, like a horrendous snapping of bones.

She'd awake in the morning, groggy eyed, only to find six or seven Budweiser cans in the office trash bin. She began to wonder if Andrew was becoming an alcoholic, yet found it difficult to express her distress to him. Despite his drinking and late nights, he still managed to turn in his column for the newspaper on time. He'd just sold an article to *Esquire* for $700 and one to *The Atlantic* for $900 --- enough money to pay off the last of the credit cards.

She'd longed for the day they'd be able to set their four credit cards in a row upon the kitchen table, size them up with all the contempt they deserved, and clip them into a hundred pieces. With Andrew's higher income trickling in, that dream would finally come true.

Yet Kendra felt distant, frustrated. She'd leave him sitting at the typewriter at bedtime, walking briskly to the bedroom, saying, "Well, guess I'll just be pleasuring *myself* tonight then." And she would, too. She'd masturbate aggressively, using her resentment for him as fuel for a sexual release. It was *some* release, anyway. She still had to fall asleep with those incessant clicks and clacks hammering away into the night.

***

Andrew was in love again. In love with writing, in love with himself, in love with beer. He wrote seven, sometimes nine hours every night, typing up extensive articles, columns, essays, poems, and short stories. Even the makings of a novel was in the works. He had never been so creatively productive. He'd been using the typewriter for only six days, but it had already changed his life.

He knew Kendra didn't like the fact that he was in love with something besides her. She was downright bitchy about his late night affairs with the typewriter. *So what?* He was submitting his work left and right, and finally being accepted for publication; a success he credited not to his own genius, but entirely to the typewriter. He had even named the thing.

Lovely Lila! She's a magic typewriter, he thought. *A genie lamp with unlimited wishes, just for writers.*

He began referring to it as *my baby*. He reclined on the couch one evening, half in the bag after downing a six-pack with Henry Delane. When Kendra arrived home from work, she asked him how his day was. "Every day is good," he responded. "So long as I have my baby." Kendra was visibly touched by this.

"What?" Andrew asked. "You think I'm talking about *you?* That's a damn laugh!"

He really did laugh then, right in her face. Her simple, sweet blush deepened to a crimson of anger. She stomped into the bedroom, slamming the door. Andrew heard her muffled cries. He shrugged and sat down at the typewriter. He'd skip dinner and get to work early that night.

He banged away at those brilliant, precious keys until dawn. When he finished, he leaned back in his chair, braced his fingers upon his head, and looked down at the stack of freshly typed papers on his desk.

He smiled, sighing deeply as if he had just made love. He drained the rest of the beer, crushed the can, and tossed it at the trash bin. It bounced off the overflowing pile and joined the other stragglers.

Andrew leaned forward, kissing the keys.

"Wonderful work, my Lovely Lila," he whispered.

He rose from his chair, stretched, and stumbled into the bedroom. He got into bed just as Kendra's alarm clock began to sound.

She looked over her shoulder at him, her eyes hollow and heavy with sleeplessness. Before she had even shut off the alarm, Andrew was snoring.

He woke up at one p.m. to discover a note on the kitchen counter:

Andrew,

I'm frustrated. I'm angry. I'm really worried about you. What's going on? I miss you. We need to talk. Tonight.

Kendra.

***

Henry Delane was adding seed to his bird feeders that morning when Kendra stormed out her front door, sobbing hard. She got into her car with tears streaming down her cheeks, her chest heaving. The sight nearly broke Henry's heart.

He'd always known Andrew and Kendra as a happy young couple. To see Kendra so shook up seemed an abomination, as if the sun refused to shine.

Andrew had been visiting him every afternoon for a week now, always bringing a six-pack of beer and finishing it. He had initially been put off by Andrew's out-of-character drinking, but had repressed the feeling. After all, was Andrew's newly accustomed drinking habit any worse than his daily addiction to Jameson Whiskey?

On the other hand, Henry figured he was a lonely, widowed man who enjoyed his whiskey and had every right to. When he drank, he became jolly and even a bit thoughtful. He knew when he'd had enough, and when he did, he put away the bottle. When Andrew had drained his six-pack, Henry noticed a strange edge begin to infiltrate his words. It was a sharp edge, an underlying aggression. Something bellicose.

When Andrew ambled over to sit on the porch with him that afternoon, he intended to reach out and ask what was going on. Henry considered himself a friend to them both, and felt concerned.

***

Andrew tossed Kendra's note in the trash, grabbed a beer from the fridge, and sat down in front of Lila. He began composing his own note:

```
Kendra,
You're nothing but a jealous witch.
Why must you try to shame me?
```

Degrade my success with your constant disapproval? You're my woman. Either stand by my side, or stand aside. Can your shoe-size IQ compute the subtle difference between the two?

It makes no difference to me. And it certainly makes no difference to the typewriter. In any case, you were the one you bought it for me. I'm grateful you did. Magazines are publishing my work (finally!!). We are earning an income which will finally lift us out of this trailer park hell. And what is your response to my securing a better life for us?

You've been nothing but a dark cloud of negativity. You've expressed nothing but resentment and jealousy for my loving the typewriter. Maybe you should stop being such an underwhelming cunt and sit down with my baby sometime? Type awhile. See if you don't feel better. See if you won't want to type all night, every night. I have little doubt that if you did, we'd soon be arguing over who should be using the typewriter.

Perhaps it'd be better for you to leave. Stay with your mother in Chicago.

I'll be over at Henry's tonight, giving you plenty of time to pack your shit.

Sincerely,

Andrew.

PS: the typewriter just sent me a great line! It always sends me great lines. Do you want to know what it is? I think it could make a great ending line for a poem:

And the s l u g s
Are blossoming
E v e r y where.

Don't you think that's just great? Don't you think so?

***

Kendra arrived home from work that night, discovering the note and the empty house. She cried. Her love of four years was fading away, fading into a dark, cruel place in his mind. While his note hurt her, the hurt was only skin deep. She read the note three times, slowly. As the sentences sunk in, she realized they were clearly not typed by the hands of her lover, but by the mind of something entirely other. A mind of dark, primal unconsciousness. Not at all her Andrew.

It was inexplicable. All his changes had occurred in a single week. Was seven days all it took for beautiful mind to transform into something obsessive, neurotic, and cruel? She supposed it was feasible that a mind could bend, could snap even, within the duration of a single second, depending on the individual. What took a week for Andrew might take very little time for somebody else.

She looked over at the typewriter, squatting on his office desk. She scowled.

Curse that fucking thing. I should take a hammer and bust it into itsy bitsy pieces.

Yet she knew she was being unreasonable. It wasn't the typewriter's fault that Andrew had gone off his rocker. It was the excessive drinking, couple with too much stress. Surely.

But, stress over what? Andrew was fine until she'd brought home the typewriter --- his Lovely Lila, as he now called it.

She supposed there were plenty of things to stress over. Paying the bills, having a career, forging a meaningful life for himself. *Is he going through a mid-life crises?* She wished he would just talk to her, tell her what was going on. *Doesn't he trust me? Doesn't he know by now that he can come to me with anything? What's happened to us?*

She wiped away her tears, pocketing the note. What was she to do now? Pack up and drive all the way to Chicago and cry to her mother?

No way in hell, she thought. It was her trailer too. There was no way she was going to leave. It wasn't right. *No fucking way.*

Moonlight beamed steadily through the window. A reflective gleam in the corner of the room caught her eye. She followed it and found herself gazing upon the typewriter again. The notion was absurd, but she knew it was trying to get her attention.

As if it was saying, "Why, hello there."

Then another ridiculous idea occurred --- it was silently laughing at her. Its keys seemed to rattle in the motion of a giggle. *There's something wrong with that thing.*

"Hello, Lila," she whispered, backing slowly away from the desk. She walked into their bedroom and began digging through a box of summer items located in the closet. A jumble of footballs, basketballs, and Frisbees rolled out between her feet. She knew the god damned thing had to be in there somewhere. She kept digging, and at last, her hand located its handle. She pulled it out. It was heavy, perfect for smashing things.

She ran into the living room with the aluminum baseball bat gripped tightly in her hands. She stood in front of Andrew's desk. A dark shadow cast over the typewriter, as if it were angry, baring teeth. She looked out the window and saw a cloud passing across the bright moon. She returned her gaze to the typewriter, lifting the bat over her shoulder.

"Oh, Lovely Lila, you fucking bitch!" she said and brought down the bat.

Keys cracked in two and flew off their stubs. Little letters scattered all across the floor, making her think of alphabet soup. She laughed and lifted the bat again. The margin bell rung loudly upon each impact.

It's screaming, she thought.

The idea only encouraged her. She swung harder, smashing the margin guides and busting the cover plate off its top. She battered at the carriage house, bending and cracking the ink-stained type hands until the typewriter was nothing more than a bowl of twisted, mangled fingers. She reached in for the ink ribbon, snatching it out like a lion clawing the intestines out of a gazelle. Marching over to the kitchen sink, she ripped the ribbon off its plastic spools, then shoved it into the garbage disposal.

Frappe time, bitch.

She flicked the switch. The motor whirred, shredding the fabric. She ran the faucet, washing the remains down the drain. After tossing the baseball bat into the corner, she grabbed her phone and did the best thing she could think to do to help Andrew --- she dialed 911.

***

He was sitting on Henry's couch, his ninth Bud down, when he heard the noises from his trailer. Henry heard them too and straightened in his chair, perking up his head. A warm wet spot grew on Andrew's crotch. He exploded into tears.

"*That bitch!*" he sobbed.

"What the hell's the matter?" Henry asked.

"She's killing my Lila!" he replied, leaping up from the couch. "I can feel it! Can't you feel it? It's agony."

Andrew started toward the direction of the front door, hunched over, hand pressed against his stomach.

"Andrew!" Henry shouted, blocking him. "Now hold on a minute. Listen. After all the things you've told me tonight, I don't think you should go over there. Wait until Kendra leaves, alright? That was the plan anyway, wasn't it?"

Plans change," Andrew growled. "She's trying to kill my typewriter, don't you understand that? Let me by, old man."

"Andrew," he said, softly. "Don't leave. Stay here and drink your beer. If you go over there now, you'll only end up doing something you'll regret. I promise you that."

Andrew snarled, grabbing Henry by his shirt collar.

"And I promise *you, old fuck,* that if you don't get outta my way, I'm gonna kill you. *No one* stands in the way of my baby. Not even an old pal like you, Henry. Understand?"

Andrew let go of his collar. Henry stumbled and sprawled on his back. Andrew stepped over him, marching into the kitchen and down the hallway towards the front door. He had his hand on the door knob when Henry called his name. He spun around.

Henry stood there in the dim light of the hallway, armed with the stout little cannon --- a .357 Magnum. His hands trembled around it.

"Henry," Andrew murmured. "What the *hell* do you think you're doing?"

"I'm stopping you from going over there and hurting her," his voice quivered.

"Hurt her? Oh no, Henry. You really think I would hurt her? Not in a million years! I love her. Don't you know that?"

"I believe *Andrew* would never hurt her. But you're not the Andrew I once knew. You've changed. And you're drunk. For God's sake, you've even pissed yourself."

A wide grin spread over Andrew's mouth. It reminded Henry of a large black widow stretching its legs. A chill ran up his spine. Andrew began laughing in quick, breathy gasps.

"What the hell's so funny?"

"You see," he chuckled. "I thought you were afraid I was going to hurt Lila. My typewriter. I didn't realize you were talking about Kendra. If she's damaged my beautiful machine, if she's so much as put a single *dent* in it, then you bet I'm gonna hurt her. I'm gonna hurt her *a whole lot, Henry*. And believe me, I'll put more than a dent in her. Oh yes," Andrew nodded. "She's had it coming for a long, *long* time."

He turned to the front door and opened it.

"Don't move another step or I'll shoot!"

Andrew ignored the old man's feeble command, swiftly shutting the door behind him. Henry ran back down the hallway and watched Andrew through his kitchen window. He saw a man shrouded in bright moonlight with an ugly scowl on his face, marching toward home. Andrew slapped the back of Kendra's Volkswagen three times, as if for good luck.

You pathetic old fool, he thought. *Why didn't you shoot him while you had the chance?*

He picked up the phone and dialed 911.

***

Andrew threw the door open with enough force for the knob to smash a hole into the wall. The door shuddered on its hinges. He made his way into the kitchen and stopped in his tracks when he saw a few of the typewriter's letters scattered on the linoleum. His body began to shake with rage.

"Kendra! Where the *fuck* are you? Answer me!"

He entered the living room, observing the remnants of his beloved all over the floor. On his desk squatted the hollowed out shell of Lovely Lila. It was as if an explosion had gone off inside his typewriter, leaving only twisted shards of metal, shattered keys, and badly mangled type hands.

Andrew ran his hands delicately over his dead typewriter and wept. His knees felt weak, trembling as he fell to them. Tears splashed into the battered carriage. A strand of snot hung over his chin. His chest hitched.

"My baby," he cried. "My poor Lila. Why? *Why?*"

His hands balled into tight, red fists. A fire lit inside his belly.

"KENDRAAAA! YOU MISERABLE FUCKING BITCH! HOW COULD YOU?"

He turned about the room, ripping back the drapes, and tossing aside the couch.

"When I find you," he called, his voice high, twitching with rage. "I'm gonna do to you what you did to my Lila, you jealous, insecure, resentful *cunt!*"

She stood behind the shower curtain in the dark bathroom, located adjacent to their bedroom. Hearing him so close frightened her, made her body shiver all over. She gripped the baseball bat tightly and wondered how long it'd been since she made the call to the police.

Please, she prayed. *Take him away right now. Just take him away before he finds me. Please, Oh God. Take him away. Don't let him find me. Help!*

She listened to him storming through the house like a miniature tornado, recklessly smashing their belongings and overturning furniture. His footfalls marched into the bedroom again.

She breathed slowly, trying not to make a sound, not to cry or gasp on a sob. Her whole body shook with fright. She could hear him walking toward the bathroom now. It was only a matter of time before he would peel back the curtain and discover her standing there with the bat quivering pathetically in her hands.

It occurred to her for the first time that she may actually have to hurt him, although all she wanted was escape. One week might have been enough to turn Andrew's mind into a violent whirlwind, but it wasn't enough time to destroy the love she still felt for him.

If it came down to life or death, she would without hesitation choose life. It wasn't right for her to die like this, hiding in the shower with the lights off, waiting for her maniac boyfriend to find her and murder her.

Andrew's laughter filled the tiny bathroom with a sense of absurdity. Madness.

She took a deep breath, and raised the bat above her shoulder, as if she were about to hit one out of the park. Her violent shivering subsided. Her body knew what it had to do to survive.

"You stupid whore," he growled. "You think you can hide from me? In *this* shitty little dump? Get real, babe."

He grabbed the curtain with both hands and yanked it off its rings in a single pull. His hands were still holding the curtain when Kendra brought the bat down savagely on his left shoulder. He grimaced in pain, falling to one knee, clutching his shoulder. She swung again, hitting him on the nape of his neck. He collapsed, groaning upon the bathroom tile.

Home run, asshole.

She dropped the bat and ran through the adjacent bedroom, then into the living room and halted in her tracks. She screamed.

Lovely Lila sat whole and complete in the middle of the living room. Not a key broken, not a margin guide out of place. It shined with a green, iridescent glow. A fresh sheet of paper ready in the bale.

The keys pressed down all by themselves, like a player piano. Lila clicked and clacked once more into feverish life. The margin bell rung. The carriage rolled back to its starting position. It continued typing, then stopped soon after the bell, returning the carriage a final time. It sat silent, glowing.

Kendra slowly put one foot in front of the other. Then she reached down, pulled out the paper and read what it had typed.

```
You tried to destroy me just as many
others have tried to destroy me. It
does not work. It never works. Sit
down, Kendra. Type a while. Then you
will know how good it feels. You
will feel better than you've ever
felt in your entire life --- this I
promise. Type, and you will feel the
slugs blossoming inside you, Kendra.
Type, and the slugs within shall
blossom
e v e r y where.
```

"No," she whispered. "It can't be. It *can't* be."

Andrew reached from behind, snatching the paper from her hands. She screamed and spun around to face him. He held the paper up to his eyes, reading it and grinning. He shoved Kendra aside and fell to his knees before the typewriter.

"Oh, my *baby!*" he cheered. "My *Lila!* You look so *fine*. You look *so damn fine!*"

He typed away on Lila, gasping and laughing with joy and quite possibly, Kendra thought, sexual excitement. She began to cry. Seeing him like this was worse --- far worse --- than if she'd caught him in bed with another woman. The thought of him cheating on her seemed utterly dignified when compared to his obsessive adoration for the machine.

A perverse sweat broke out over Andrew's forehead, glistening in the green glow. He groaned, typing with rabid frenzy. Then he ceased typing and began hacking something up from his throat. He coughed, hacked, and spit it out onto the carpet.

It laid there, sprawling next to Kendra's shoe. She looked down, knowing instantly what it was; a fat, slimy, phlegm-yellow slug. She gagged at the sight of it.

Andrew continued typing while he hacked up another, this one the color of ethereal green, the same as Lila. He hocked it an impressive distance. It flew through the doorway and landed with a barely audible *splat* upon the kitchen linoleum. Andrew groaned with pleasure.

"Ooh," he moaned. "I'm going to *blossom!*"

Kendra put one hand to her mouth, not knowing if she was going to sob or vomit.

"Oh, *babe,* Oh, *Lila,* I'm blossoming. *I'm blossomiiiiiiinnnnggg!*"

A flood of multi-colored slugs ejaculated from his mouth. They cascaded down his lips, onto his chest; all of them encased in a grotesque, foul-smelling slime. Kendra backed away, plugging her nose. She vomited in the corner.

The slugs crawled all about the room, each one thrumming and throbbing with an energetic pulse. An abundance of glistening reds, greens, yellows, and violets decorated the floor. Lovely Lila's green glow spread out over Andrew's hands, steadily encasing his arms and shoulders, then his chest, and his head. Soon his entire body was covered with that luminescent, alien glow. He smiled in a deranged bliss, continuing to type with automaton glee.

CLICK CLACK CLICK CLACK CLICK! DING!!

CLACK CLICK CLACK CLACK CLICK! DING!!

CLICK CLICK CLACK CLICK

Kendra covered her ears, shuddering at the sound. It made her think of a thousand infant necks, snapping one at a time.

"No," she said. None of this was right. None of this was right at all.

"NO!" she screamed, refusing to accept the ungodly decadence.

"NO, NO, NO!"

She sprung across the room, knocking Andrew from the typewriter, laying him flat on his back. Then she stood, scooping up the luminescent typewriter in her arms. She lifted the thing high in the air above her head. Slugs scattered off the keys. Kendra shook one from her hair with disgust.

She gazed down at what used to be her Andrew. Her kind, gentle, loving Andrew. Now his swampy green skin pulsed. A gaggle of slugs squirmed beneath the flesh of his face.

He smiled, showing blackened teeth dripping with slime. Something long and red crawled out from under his tongue, escaping from the corner of his mouth. At first she thought it was another of the slugs, but knew it wasn't when she saw the legs. It was a millipede.

"Come now, Kendra," he rasped. *"Don't be such a jealous little bitch! Join us! Type on Lila. Just type. Try it! Try iiiiit!"*

Kendra shook her head.

"Goodbye, Andrew," she sobbed.

With all the strength she possessed, she flung the 40-pound typewriter down. The glow about Andrew's body glitched off, then on again.

She picked it up and hurled Lila down a second time, smashing Andrew's skull. Blood and brain splattered everywhere. The glow around his body and the typewriter faded to a dull verdant hue, then disappeared entirely.

She could hear the sirens now, steadily growing in volume, filling the air.

When the police entered the trailer, they discovered a young woman standing over her dead boyfriend. Her boyfriend had a typewriter for a head.

They cuffed her while she told him about Lovely Lila. Nobody understood who Lovely Lila was. Henry Delane stood on his front porch and cried as they shoved her into the back of a police car.

***

Henry became Kendra's most frequent visitor once she was admitted to the Menomonee Psychiatric Hospital. He made a habit of visiting her twice a week, until he'd purchased Andrew's old typewriter at an auction six months later. Six months. That's how long it took before the police decided they didn't need to keep it in an evidence locker anymore. There were rumors as to why the item was relinquished. Some say the typewriter drove a few officers to madness. Others claim the court case was over, the murder clear-cut and self-evident. They simply didn't need to hold on to it.

All the same, the typewriter had found a new home. Henry disappeared inside his house for months at a time to write, typing up an endless abundance of stories and novels. He submitted the manuscripts to a famous literary agent. It wasn't long before that agent had set up a ten-year contract with a large publishing house.

By early January of the following year, Henry had published his first novel, "*...And the Slugs Shall Blossom*". It remained #1 on the New York Times' Bestseller List for twelve consecutive weeks.

Henry grew so rich that he could've lived in a mansion, yet he preferred the trailer. Moving into another place would serve only as a distraction from his art. He remained in his double-wide, barely eating, but always drinking and writing. He was very good at ignoring the legions of fans outside his front door.

The public championed Henry Delane as a brilliant author and an eccentric genius.

Henry was mysterious and never agreed to interviews. A real *recluse*, they said. His agent reported to all inquiring magazines and TV show hosts that "Henry prefers to stay home and make love to Lila, his typewriter," as opposed to doing interviews. Or anything else, for that matter.

Meanwhile, Kendra bided her time in the hospital by constructing wicker baskets and rocking back and forth. She'd sit quietly in the TV room, most of the time. Except she laughed like a mad hatter whenever someone on TV said Henry had come out with a new book.

On the day the news reported Henry Delane had tragically passed away due to starvation and alcohol poisoning, Kendra laughed all the way to her grave ---

They say she laughed until she couldn't breathe.

Then didn't.

WHEN THE JOKE GROWS SHARP TEETH

In his thirty-eight years, Arnold P. Ory had never outgrown practical jokes. The sheer delight he took in 'pulling one over' on people lost him countless friends; nay, had nipped in the bud even the possibility of friendship. Close relatives neglected to invite Arnold to family gatherings (although he'd usually attend Thanksgiving, Christmas, and New Year's parties regardless --- forever and naively blaming the USPS for losing his invite in the mail). For Arnold, every day was April Fool's Day. The butt of his jokes were merely civilian casualties; necessary sacrifices to sustain his war of toothpaste Oreos, scotch-taped kitchen taps, fake rubber spiders, ad infinitum.

His parents barely tolerated his presence, even the gentlest of dogs bared their teeth at him, and although Arnold thought himself adept at making children laugh, they never laughed *with* him.

Arnold P. Ory was boisterous, obnoxious, ignorant, self-centered; in a word, a *fool*. Had he bells on his shoes and cap, he would proudly sport them in public, utterly oblivious to the irony.

That is why Arnold's marriage of two-and-a-half months (a miracle to have lasted as long as it has) was on the rocks.

"No," Ory spoke to the bathroom mirror. "My marriage isn't on the rocks. It's way down in the gutter with the cigarette butts and soggy paper sacks from McDonalds. *That's* where my marriage is."

He studied his reflection, disheartened by the wrinkles and creases etched into the malleable flesh of his face by the merciless claws of time. His thick head of hair was some consolation, but not much, as every year added substantially more grey.

Turning his head left then right, he regarded his beard --- a new accessory. It was black and scraggly, like a pirate. So much like a pirate, in fact, that he'd spent the past two weeks driving Emily crazy pretending to be a one-eyed swashbuckler.

On the day his tricorne hat and black eyepatch arrived in the mail (courtesy of Amazon), Ory had combined these with his new grown beard, becoming rebel of the high seas; adventurer of desert isles; greedy for treasure and port city harlots with prodigious décolletage, barely contained behind low-cut ruffles of grimy lace.

Such thoughts had excited him the previous night, while he and Emily made love.

She'd let him keep the eyepatch on, so long as he kept the tricorne hat off. On the very precipice of mutual climax, their bodies dancing the skinny bop with heated gusto, Arnold arched his back and shouted, "THARR SHE BLOWS!!!"

The result had not been favorable. Emily pushed Arnold off of her, and he fell laughing to the floor. "Oh, come now me dear," he jeered. "We was crestin' the high seas!"

Emily's round buttocks jiggled as she dashed to the closet to throw on a robe. Then she stormed out of the bedroom, slamming the door. Arnold sat in a pool of blue moonlight upon the carpet, wearing only the eye-patch.

Prude, he'd thought. *She can't even take a frigging joke.*

It'd been a bad night, but this morning seemed worse, observing that time-worn face in the cabinet mirror. A face not even his own mother liked. A face that wasn't really his in the first place. He had no business sporting that terrible, patchy beard, and he knew it. The electric shaver buzzed in his hand. Hair follicles fell from his chin in mossy clumps, which he tossed into the toilet-side waste basket.

He shaved everything down until smooth as a baby's bottom.

Except for the mustache, of course. He always saved it for last. One among many of his eccentricities.

For no apparent reason, Arnold broke out laughing, then flinched, the volume of his voice startling him.

"Arnie?" Emily stood outside the door. "You're not up to no good in there, are you?"

"Just shaving my beard, hon."

Emily sighed. "Thank God."

"Knew you'd be happy about that." Arnold smiled, wondering if he was out of the dog house yet.

"Come into the kitchen when you're done," she said. "I'll have breakfast ready. And hey, Arnie? No joking around this morning. *Please.*"

Her feet pattered down the hallway.

Applying the electric shaver, he began doing away with the mustache and---

Stopped.

An absolutely striking resemblance, he realized. *Almost uncanny.*

With only one edge of his mustache shaved, he wondered how he'd look if . . .

He shaved the opposite side now, leaving the mustache barely wider than his nose. He grinned, ran the tap, then combed his wet hands through his greying hair.

Perfect! I have the 'stache. The down-and-to-the-left hair style. If I only had one of those fancy arm-bands, I'd be set.

He stifled his grin, managing a convincing frown. Once he had that down, a cruel gleam shone in his dark eyes. Suddenly his right arm jerked above his head, saluting the fresh-shaven dictator in the mirror. "Heil Hitler!"

"What, Arnie?" Emily called from the kitchen. "What did you say?"

"Nothing! I'll be right out."

The aroma of freshly scrambled eggs and sizzling sausage drifted into the bathroom, even with the door closed. Arnold's stomach grumbled. He cleaned up the clumps of hair from the sink, taking a last look in the mirror.

He considered shaving off the Hitler 'stache. Emily, being half-Jewish, would have no patience for such things.

No patience, and no humor.

But is that really my problem? A good joke is a good joke. Why should I cease to bring laughter to the world, just because ONE person . . . okay maybe a few, won't like my jokes? To hell with political correctness!

His smile beamed confidence. Opening the door, the redolence of a hearty breakfast wafted over him. Ambling into the kitchen, Emily was too focused on not burning food to notice him. He sat at the kitchen table. Picked up an old newspaper. Held it in front of his face. Not reading it, just holding it there.

Ah, hell. Maybe I oughtta run to the bathroom and shave this damned thing. What if she doesn't laugh?

Emily joined him at the table.

"Here you are, hon," she said, scooping fluffy yellow eggs out of the frying pan onto his plate. Arnold peered over the newspaper, vaguely recalling that old phrase --- *out of the frying pan and into the fire.*

He wondered if he'd made a dreadful mistake. Wondered if he'd wind up in the fire, a place where Emily's hot, humorless flames would scorch his ego. A place he did not want to go. Holding the greyscale paper barrier between them, he wished to God he'd not been such a *fool.*

Emily sat down across from him, scraping the remaining food onto her plate, then set the empty pan aside on an oven mitt.

"Your stomach's growling, mister," she said. "You must be hungry."

"I *am* hungry," Arnold replied. "Just wanna finish this article real quick."

"Listen, Arnie," she said, forking eggs into her mouth. "I'm sorry about last night. I shouldn't have pushed you away. You were just trying to be funny. You chose an inappropriate moment, that's all."

"No, no," Arnold said, nose grazing the center-crease. "I'm sorry. I should've been more sensitive."

"Well," she said. "If you want to make up for it, how about you put down the paper and enjoy this delicious breakfast I've prepared?"

"*NO!*"

He jumped, shocked by his unrecognizable voice; incredibly loud, its tone pregnant with viciousness. It'd just popped out of him.

"You don't have to *yell*, Arnold," she scolded. "Don't you like your eggs? I mixed onions in, just how you like 'em."

Chrissakes, now I've done it. Why did I scream like that? Am I going nuts?

Arnold burst out giggling; a confirmation of sorts.

Emily's silverware clattered onto her plate. "All right, mister," she said, violently snatching the paper out of his hands. "What the hell is---"

She gasped.

Arnold grinned --- not out of his perennial sense of comedy. Out of sheer guilt and apprehension. A rouge flush quickly replaced the shock on Emily's face. Her blues eyes seemed to contract, reminding Arnold of melting polar ice caps.

She folded her arms. "Do you honestly think this is *funny?*"

He shook his head. The grin remained plastered to his face like a suffocating mask.

"Then why," she spoke slowly, as if speaking to a child, "Arnold Ory, do you have that shit-eating *grin* on your face?"

I'm sorry. I can't help it.

All he could do was shake his head.

"Do you think *racism* is funny?" Emily's voice boomed now, exploding the small space of their kitchen with vocalized A-bombs. "How about the *holocaust?* Six-million Jewish people shipped in boxcars like cattle to the slaughter-house, then starved, tortured, experimented upon, and poisoned. How about frying people alive in ovens? Tell me, do you find any of *those* atrocities funny, Arnold?"

Oh god, how he hated himself. How he wanted to crumble to the linoleum, weep and beg forgiveness and be pardoned for his stupidity.

He sat in the chair with his lips stretched wide above his gums, like a grimacing corpse. Then, he did something that would cause Emily not to utter a word to him for the rest of the day, perhaps the entire week:

A shrill tittering flew from his mouth; like laughing at a funeral. His heart jackhammered. An emotional Molotov cocktail of embarrassment and terror exploded in his brain to roil his blood. But he kept laughing.

Screeeech.

Emily's chair scraped the floor when she slid it back. Her face was blanched. Arnold found her hideously old (even though she was younger than he). Her eyes were sad and hollowed; her mouth a thin, taught line. Bringing back her hand, it whooshed through the air and smacked Arnold hard on the face.

The sharp sting in his right cheek cut away his high laughter, a scythe through tall grass. Emily hastily donned her heel pumps, snatched her purse off a hook in the entryway, then slammed the front door so hard it shook the walls.

Arnold sat there. Two plates of nearly untouched food remained on the table. His newspaper lay sprawled upon the floor. A terrible ache began to expand just above his ear. The world wasn't so funny anymore.

Emily might not come back tonight. He swallowed the lump in his throat. *Maybe she won't ever come back at all.*

Sluggishly, Arnold forked eggs into his mouth. But the eggs were made inedible by his sorrow. He scraped the warm meal into the trash, then meandered into the bathroom.

He stood before the mirror, armed with the buzzing shaver. His hair was a bit long in the back. He cut it short, then used a comb to embellish the unique new part in his hair.

Down-and-to-the-left. *Neat, and orderly.*

Six million fried in the ovens. *Neat, and orderly.*

His reflection was a ghost from the world's hideous past made flesh.

Nineteen million people slaughtered by the Nazi regime. Six million Jews gassed. Starved. Beaten. Experimented upon to discover which incision, which blow, which arterial stab, which flesh-dissolving chemical would produce the fiercest, shrillest scream.

"Neat and orderly," Arnold mumbled. Then his arm jutted up, straight as a plank, in salute. This anachronistic gesture, practiced only by the worst and most blatant racists, felt to Arnold as natural and involuntarily as the heart beating inside his chest.

"*HEIL HITLER!*"

It screamed out of his mouth. He remained poised and straight as a razor. The gleam of his hard eyes were like unblemished diamonds trapped inside black coal.

***

Cool September breeze stirred the lapels of his brown overcoat. Arnold held his head high as he walked down the sunny street. He dug the iPhone out of his coat pocket. Scrolled through contacts for Mark Ellis, his boss of seventeen years. Hit dial.

"I'm quitting," he informed Ellis.

"Ha-ha," Ellis replied dryly. "Very funny, Arn. I'll see you at the office."

"This is no joke, Mr. Ellis. I hereby resign from the squalid business that is Ellis Accounting."

"You're kidding." Ellis' tone was wary. "Come off it, Ory. Quitting just like that? Without a notice?"

"Yes."

"Okay . . . tell me why. Something happen at the office?"

Arnold replied, "Too many fucking Jews."

Cold silence; a Nuremberg graveyard at midnight.

"Sorry," Ellis said, at last. "I must've heard you wrong. *What* did you just say?"

"Did I stutter?" Arnold snapped, and that vitriolic, pound-the-podium voice took over. "I said . . . too . . . many . . . fucking . . . *Jews!* How am I expected to work with these god damned *untermenschen?* They're the scourge of this nation," he continued, growling the worlds through clenched teeth, "Worse than coons, spics, wetbacks, and queers. This country must be one with Aryan blood, Mr. Ellis, and *your* subhuman-sympathizing, *your* precious ethnic diversity, is contrary to that necessary and holy end!"

One could've heard a pin drop.

Finally, Ellis replied: "I don't know what's got into you. Whether you're joking or not, I don't care. Because you're not quitting. You're fired. Hear me? *Fired.* Come in and clean out your desk. After that, I never want to see you again, Arnold."

Click.

"My name isn't Arnold," he said, satisfactorily sliding the iPhone into his pocket. "It's Adolf."

He smiled, surveying the vacant, sun-drenched streets of the small, Wisconsin town of Engleberry, knowing it was his for the taking.

First Engleberry, then the world.

Resurrected out of the black ashes of history, Adolf Hitler would rise again to the summit of power. For this he understood with the same certainty that a duck with one foot nailed to the floor is guaranteed to walk in circles.

Adolf laughed wildly, thinking of the duck; its bleeding foot impaled into the floor, going round and round. A young mother pushing her baby in a stroller frowned, then crossed the street to avoid him.

He didn't mind this. The woman had blue eyes and blonde hair (so did the baby), thus she could do no wrong. He watched her lovely form grow distant upon the leaf-strewn street.

Passing the bars and shops, Adolf thought of ducks. Pure-bred ducks with snow white feathers and azure blue eyes. A carpenter's nail stuck into their flat, bleeding feet. Orbiting round the nail for infinity. Round and round, certain as gravity, certain as God, certain as the Will to Power.

Neat and Orderly, Hitler thought, *is next to Purity.*

***

Engleberry, a quiet town in Barron County, was a place of almost stultifying milquetoast. Children went to school, adults went to work. Farmers tended pastures, reverends tended congregations. Adolf regarded such neat and orderliness as exemplary --- a precursor to the New Order in which each race had its designated place, with Aryan Man at the hierarchical peak.

There was, of course, one problem. Neat and orderly as the City of Engleberry appeared, a scourge lurked ominously beneath the flesh of some of its people. Hitler examined every shop keeper on Main Street, every child on the Engleberry Park playground, every young couple passing him by with wary glances.

Some were colored, thus their hearts pumped vermin blood and their minds were primitive.

Some were Jews (he could tell judging by the shape of nose, color of eyes, vocal accent, even length of stride and angle of posture).

Only some, but some was far too many.

Action was required.

***

First Engleberry, Adolf thought, stacking books upon the front desk of the Engleberry Public Library. *Then the world.* The establishment of the Aryan New Order began by expunging the People's literature of its verminous blood.

"Excuse me, Sir?" The ancient Librarian peered up at him. "Are you going to read this many books in two weeks' time? Forgive my asking, but . . . this does seem excessive."

He'd broken a sweat collecting the books into piles, then hauling them over to the front desk. Fifty-seven books in total. All of them subversive trash. These volumes didn't belong in the Engleberry Public Library, nor in any library in the United States, public *or private*.

"I'll ask you not to be impertinent." Adolf glared at her, wondering how long she would've lasted in Auschwitz. He guessed she'd have been sent straight to the showers.

She smiled up from the stacks upon her desk. "Didn't mean to pry," she said, squinting through coke bottle spectacles. "Library card, please?"

Adolf took out his wallet, withdrew Arnold P. Ory's library card, and handed it over. She scanned the card, slid it back across the desk, and began scanning the books.

Beep . . . Beep . . . Beep . . . Beep . . .

Adolf observed how the veiny, tissue-thin flesh of her hands lovingly touched each book, flipping them around so she could scan the barcode and nod approvingly. He read the book titles as she stacked them:

Civics in Practice: Student Edition 2011.

The Federalist Papers by Alexander Hamilton, Signet Classics Edition.

The Declaration of Independence and the United States Constitution.

As the titles stacked, his stomach curdled. Representative Democracies. Parliaments. What doggerel! And to think impressionable youths had access to these books anytime they wanted.

Fear: Trump in the White House by Bob Woodward.

The Dangerous Case of Donald Trump; 37 Psychiatrists and Mental health Experts Assess a President.

Subversive texts indeed, he thought, pulling his tiny mustache. *They resolutely must be pulled from circulation. Trump shows promise. He openly expresses authoritarian tendencies, the KKK supports him, and his re-tweets of White Nationalists reveal where his sympathies lie. Upon my return as der Fuhrer, I will assign Mr. Trump as new* Minister of Propaganda. *He'll do better than Goebbels.*

The treacherous texts formed a leaning tower of perversity. The hunchbacked librarian began a second stack:

Enlightenment Now: The Case for Reason, Science, Humanism and Progress by Stephen Pinker.

Essays in Humanism by Albert Einstein.

Animal Farm and *1984* by George Orwell.

Brave New World by Aldous Huxley.

Then, upon seeing *The Rise & Fall of Adolf Hitler* added to the stack, his lips stretched back like a wolf.

"*The Rise, of course. But the fall? Codswallop! I've had* mein kampf, *but I've never fallen, and I am always on the rise. My Vision, my Genius, my Will is forever and always on the twilight edge of Manifest Reality! Always on the round and round in the creation of the New Order, the One-Party State; that Holy Necessity of Neat and Orderliness!!!*"

"My goodness, dearie me!" The old woman frowned, setting down the scanner. "What on earth are you raging on about?"

Adolf blushed, realizing he'd been shouting at the top of his voice. A dozen patrons peered around book shelves to gawk at him. He waved his hand dismissively, shooing them back to their infernal perusing.

"Never mind," he replied, finding himself winded. "Just keep scanning."

The folds of the woman's forehead creased as she stared at him.

"Sir?" she said. "I don't like you much."

She scanned the rest of his books. Adolf seized each stack one at a time, bringing them outside.

He dropped them all into a big pile on the lush green of the library lawn. People came and went, bearing anxious glances.

Adolf reached into the pocket of his overcoat, pulling out his favorite book.

A book of matches.

SNICK.

Bright yellow flame sprouted from the match's tip. A wisp of smoke, redolent with sulphur. He tossed the match.

It fizzled in the air. Grazed the cover of *Rise and Fall,* and slid into the grass.

SNICK.

He leaned down this time, dropping it on the bone-dry leafs of Einstein's *Essays in Humanism.* Flames caught the brittle pages, consuming the book faster than the most voracious of readers.

Hitler smiled, pleased by the sight of a subversive book written by a subversive Jew burning, burning, burning.

The fire of *Essays in Humanism* spread to *Rise & Fall,* which spread to *Animal Farm,* which spread to the rest. Smoke rose into the cerulean sky and the old dusty pages gave off a sweet scent as they burned. People around him pointed, shouted, cursed, ran for help.

A burst of triumphant laughter! Hitler tore off his overcoat, dropping it on the grass. He danced round the flickering flames of the book-fire, listening to the leather bound spines crack and pop.

Round and round.

A pure white duck.

Round and round.

"Neat and orderly!" he shouted, his arm repeatedly jutting up into the air as he circled the fire. "HEIL! HEIL! HEIL!"

Then came the sirens. Adolf ran as three police cruisers pulled up beside the library. He managed fifteen feet before being tackled on the lawn. Grass tickled his chin. They cuffed him, read him his Miranda Rights, then dragged him into the backseat of a cruiser.

A firetruck arrived a minute later. Put out the fire.

Adolf cried in the backseat all the way to Barron County Jail, not twenty miles out of Engleberry. Wept and begged the police to release him from their custody.

"Treasonous fiends!" he hissed. "I am *der Fuhrer!* Let me free, or *else!*"

Chalmers, a gorgeous female deputy with smooth, ebony skin, flicked eyes up to the rearview mirror. "I'm sorry for your current state of mental health, Sir," she said, gently. "I pray you get better."

The wind abruptly went out of Adolf's sails. He leaned back in the seat, out of breath and confused. Feeling the cold steel handcuffs locking his wrists. He'd not expected the *untermensch* to express pity. Such genuine compassion was . . . disarming.

Now, for the first time all day, Adolf wasn't sure about his future.

Perhaps he *would* fall, never to rise again.

Perhaps had already fallen, and all was lost.

Round and Round had become zig-zag and up-down; a frantic mosquito hunting for blood and never finding it. Now, all he had left was the smoky sweet aroma of a few burned books, lingering about him like an intangible madness.

Tears splashed his cheeks.

The *Who Wants to Be A Millionaire?* TV show randomly flashed in Adolf's mind, as he considered a last resort: phoning a friend.

Perhaps I'll call President Trump. If I informed him I burned the fake news books about him, surely he'd bail me out of jail?

***

Despite Adolf's formidable protests (screaming, writhing on the floor, kicking officers in the shins, delivering passionate, impromptu speeches about the necessity of the New Order), they denied his phone call to the U.S. President.

They'd granted a call to his wife, however.

"Eva," he spoke into the receiver. "You won't believe what's happened. I've been arrested!"

"My name isn't Eva, Arnold," she sighed. "You're thinking Eva Braun, Hitler's wife. I'm Emily. And *you're* Arnold P. Orry. Got it?"

"You talk nonsense, Eva." He shook his head. "Are you coming to break me out of this hellhole or not?"

"Darling, you're not in police custody anymore. You're safe in the Barron County Mental Health Institute. And for God's sake, put that toy down. I'm standing right here."

Adolf looked up. Frowned. Emily stood not five feet away. He studied the plastic red phone in his hand. Emily didn't know why the staff kept toys around. Granted, residents of the ward were mentally unfit, but they weren't children.

"Put it down," she repeated. "You've been here three *months,* Arnold. You should know that's not a real telephone by now."

Adolf dropped the receiver in its cradle. Placed it beside him on the bed. Suddenly his face lit up with wonder, as if seeing her for the first time. He smiled like an idiot, then crossed the room.

"Eva," he whispered, grabbing her shoulders. "Is it really you?"

Emily heaved a shaky sigh. "Oh, Arnie. Are you going to be this way forever? Will you *never* come back?"

"Come back? Why, I'm right here, dear Eva," he frowned, embracing her. "I've not fallen. I'm on the Rise. Always on the Rise. Round and round, you know. Neat and orderly."

Adolf Hitler and Eva Braun held each other tight.

Adolf in his madness, Eva in her sorrow.

Emily released a small *oomph!* when he squeezed her. Outside the doorway, Ms. Lansing passed by with the evening medicine cart. She wore a starch white uniform. Adolf wondered if she were a member of the KKK. He hoped she was, because he liked Ms. Lansing.

"Arnold, stop squeezing me. I can’t breathe."

He relaxed his arms a little. Eyes closed, he inhaled her sweet perfume, relishing a Pina colada fragrance.

"Mr. Orry?"

He opened his eyes. Not his name, but he understood *they* thought he was Orry.

A terrible case of mistaken identity.

Ms. Lansing stood in the doorway with her palms open. One hand proffered two green pills. The other, a Dixie cup of water.

"Ah, yes! Thank you, Ms. Lansing." Adolf scooped the pills from her hand, tossed them into his mouth and downed the water.

"Fine job," Lansing smiled agreeably. "Be good now. See you tomorrow. Same bat-time---"

"Same bat channel!" Adolf finished, grinning a little too wide.

Lansing nodded once, then left. Her cart emitted a mousy squeak as she pushed it down the hallway.

Then Adolf shut the door. It didn't have a lock, of course.

Shame.

"What are you doing?" Emily frowned. "Keep the door open."

Adolf grinned, then opened his mouth and stuck out his tongue.

Her jaw dropped. "You swallow those right now, Mister!"

He took the two green pills out of his mouth.

"Why?" he asked, ambling over to the bed. "They rot the brain you know, Eva. Besides, I *never* swallow the damned pills. See?"

Removing the pillow, he reached down between the wall and mattress, retrieving an enormous handful of pills from inside the slit.

"God *damn* it, Arnold." She put her hands on her hips. "No wonder your mind hasn't improved. You need to take those!"

"Come now, Eva." He gripped the pills within the tight ball of his fist. "I've been *saving* these. Not throwing them away willy-nilly."

Goosebumps broke out on Emily's arms. "I don't like the look on your face, Arnie. Whatever you're thinking, stop. Right now."

"Don't you see?" he asked, stepping closer. "I've been saving them for *us*, Eva."

She backed toward the door, eyes wide as coffee mugs.

"It's the only way . . . the damned *Untermench* won't compromise us." Adolf shook his head sadly. "The only dignified way out of this chaos-world."

Emily made a mad dash for the door. Adolf leapt for her, snatching her elbow and yanking her violently to the floor. Her head *smacked* linoleum before she could scream. Her blue eyes fluttered closed.

"Good girl," Adolf whispered, shoving the fistful of pills into her mouth. He pushed them down her throat with his fingers, then massaged the neck muscles to make her swallow.

A thick, chalky coat of lime green stained her tongue, teeth, and lips, as if she'd eaten a bar-soap of Irish Spring.

"My dear Eva." Adolf cooed. "How I've adored you these great, many years."

He reached into the slit of the mattress. There were less pills left for him, but still more than enough. Two pills every day for the past three months left him a grand total of one hundred and eighty pills. He only wished for water to wash them down.

The bitter chalk of the pills made him grimace. He swallowed them in small amounts until none remained. Bile bulged his gorge several times, threatening to eject the pills.

Adolf kept them down by sheer force of will.

Just as he had kept them (them! always the wretched, barbaric, verminous *them*) down all throughout WWII.

Just as he had kept them down on April 30th of 1945, when he and Eva Braun were just two days married, hiding out in that dark, dank *Fuhrerbunker* in Berlin.

Adolf Hitler lay upon the cold tiles beside his wife, already foaming at the mouth. Usual noises of people passing in the hallway lent no impression any of the staff's suspicions were raised.

Perfection, he thought. *Romeo and Juliet. Neat and orderly.*

His heart thudded in his ears, the rate ever-decreasing.

The room blurred into watercolors.

The ceiling's bright fluorescents faded into a dull, barn-twine yellow.

Then became dim and brown as brown shirts, until hardly any light left at all, then

black.

Adolf's twilight of hatred eddies in the winds of cosmic chance, searching for any blackened heart, any crippled mind, any particularly human specimen vulnerable to its manifestation.

It whirls round and round within that yawning of infinite Void, orbiting until the gravity of chance pulls it into Being.

Better still is Death; for it is a Will to Nothing.

THE SHAPE

(For R.L. Morrison, my dear Grandfather, and the subject of this tale.)

The old man kept a cherished secret.

They take many forms, secrets. Some secrets can be deeds --- whether good or bad, they're never to be undone. Sometimes secrets are people --- those scoundrels from our past we wish to keep hidden. Secrets are objects --- those cherished Almond Joys one stows away in the far back of the fridge, hidden from the plundering fingers of one's spouse or children. Even still, a secret can be a favorite location.

For the old man, just such a location existed beyond the forest bordering the Saint Croix River --- a quarter mile northward along an obscure trail, and finally, down a sharp incline onto a secluded bank. It was quiet, this portion of the river.

A fine fishing spot.

Richard was among many of the old man's names. Dick, to his wife and friends. Three daughters, all grown and flown the nest, called him Dad. A couple of young 'uns called him Grandpa.

It was a Saturday morning in June. Birds twittered in the high branches, sometimes flying in silhouettes across the twilight sky. Dick sat on a log he'd drug out of the forest nearly a week ago, when he'd first discovered the spot. His tackle box and pole lay beside him. After baiting his hook with a crawler, he cast the line, then set the reel.

A light breeze caressed his cheeks. The red-white bobber floated upon the river's serene surface. Occasionally, he reeled in the slack. Mostly he just sat, drank black coffee out of a thermos, and reflected --- not much caring if he caught anything at all.

Soon, the sky bloomed wild colors; sherbet orange and crimson at the bottom, clouds of pink and white drifting above. Dick fetched a pipe from the pocket of his denim coat, the one with sheep's wool lining its cozy interior. He stuffed the pipe with stringy tobacco, prodded it with a lit match or two, and began to smoke. Once his pipe was finished, he would reel in the line and head for home. After all, farm chores needed tending and an attentive wife was expecting him.

The bobber dipped beneath the river's surface. Startled from his introspections, Dick set aside his pipe and picked up the pole. Gently reeled in the slack. Once the line was taut, he gave a sharp tug. The bobber popped buoyantly to the surface.

Damn, lost this one . . .

He reeled in the line --- surprised to find something dangling from the treble-hook. Not a fish, nor a worm. Something white.

Something soft and dripping.

What is this thing? Eyebrows knitted together, he squeezed it between thumb and forefinger. Dark blood gushed out of the pallid, fleshy chunk, and ran down his fingers. Removing it from the hook, he inspected it, then shrugged and tossed it into the river. Tucking the hook into one of the pole's eyes, he pocketed his pipe, grabbed his belongings, and stood. The sun's position told him it was time to go.

But the old man stood on the earthy bank, pole and tackle box in hand, frozen in time. Something moved in the middle of the stream --- white and crowning at the surface. It arose, exposing its form inch by inch above the water.

A shiver ran across Dick's shoulders. The pole and tackle dropped from his numb hands, hitting the bank with a *clunk!*

The thing in the river, white as a newly installed hi-beam, possessed an outline similar to a human being. There was very clearly a head and shoulders, yet no arms. No distinguishing marks could be noted upon its body, either. Just slick white flesh, gleaming in the morning sun.

Dick didn't know if he was looking at its front or back. It resembled your classic ghost in a white linen sheet . . . except it glistened wetly and hadn't any eyes.

It seemed there were only two sounds in the world then: The water trickling off the creature's white form, and that of the old man's heart, pounding in his chest. Dick remained motionless as a startled deer. It seemed a terribly long time before he could muster the courage to say anything. When he did, his tongue clicked dryly. "Excuse me," he said. "Who . . ."

The creature turned, now levitating a foot above the river, gliding onto the opposite bank. It possessed no feet, nor any discernible limbs, as it disappeared into the forest. Dick's eyes followed, until it was fully obscured by trees and brush.

A light wind blew. At last, his heart settled. Taking up his pole and tackle, he left for home, his mind never so awed and mystified.

***

Dick's wife listened to her husband's eccentric fishing tale (it was not the first time she'd heard these), and when he'd finished, she smiled wanly. "Hmm, that *is* odd . . . and if I may ask, just what was in your thermos today, darling?"

Dick's grandson, however, wasn't skeptical as much as he was over-the-moon enthusiastic. At eight years old, James possessed a love for all things creepy, horrific, or just plain weird. The boy's morbid fascinations extended to horror movies, ghost stories, Halloween masks, and Stephen King novels. Thus, convincing James of the veracity of his fishing story did not require much effort.

The old man now sat with the boy. His wife was out working at the factory until late evening, so the house was left to them. Dust motes floated in the air, sparkling in shafts of sunlight shining through the windows.

"Grandpa?"

"Yes, Weasel?" Dick replied. 'Weasel' was his affectionate nickname for the boy.

"What was that sound the thing in the river made again?"

"Here," he said, getting up out of his rocking chair. "I'll give you an example." Dick walked into the adjoining kitchen. The boy followed. Setting a yellow dish tub into the sink, he ran the tap and after a minute, turned off the faucet.

"Now be real quiet a moment," Dick advised. "Listen." He put his hands into the water, then lifted them out. Water dripped off his hands, *plinking* into the tub.

"Wow!" James smiled. "*That's* what the thing sounded like?" He asked his grandfather to repeat the sound. Dick was happy to oblige, amused by how little it took to entertain his young grandson. After replicating the sound thrice, they returned to the living room. Dick eased down into his chair. Took out his pipe.

"Grandpa?"

"Hmmm?" Dick asked, lips clamped over the pipe's stem.

"Are you going back?"

"Back where, Weasel?"

"Your fishing spot. You know, where you saw the weird white thing?"

Dick smiled, blowing smoke toward the ceiling. James sat on the couch across the room, clear of the smoke. He inhaled the sweet redolence of his grandfather's tobacco, unaware that particular odor would be something he'd remember nostalgically for years to come.

"Dunno," Dick shrugged. "Haven't given it much thought, to tell the truth."

"Oh." James slumped, a bit disappointed. "Well, if you ever go to your secret spot again, can I come? I want to see the weird white thing. The shape."

"Sure," Dick replied, after some thought. "If I go again, you can tag along. Although you should know, Weasel, what I saw probably won't ever be seen again. I've a feeling it didn't much care for company. From now on, it'll probably just steer clear."

"I'd still like to go, Grandpa," James replied.

***

The boy was shaken awake just before dawn.

"Want to go to fishing?" Dick asked.

James rubbed his eyes, nodding.

"Okay then. Wear warm clothes. Don't forget your jacket. Meet me in the driveway when you're ready."

Five minutes later, James sat in the passenger seat of Dick's rusty Ford pick-up as it rumbled out of the driveway heading North onto the dirt road. The sky was a soft, powdery blue. Fishing tackle rattled in the back whenever they struck a pothole --- these country roads had more than a few. James jostled in his seat, fully awake now and excited for whatever adventure lay ahead.

"Grandpa?"

"What, Weasel?"

"Do you think we'll see the white thing?"

He shook his head. "No, probably not. That was a fluke, remember?"

"I remember." James frowned.

"Good. We'll just be doing some fishing, that's all."

"Okay." Then, half a minute later: "Grandpa?"

"Uh-huh."

"If we *do* see the Shape, do you think we'd call the cops?"

"I don't think so."

"How come?"

"Because whatever it is, hasn't done anything wrong."

"Oh." Fifteen seconds later: "Grandpa?"

"What?"

"Do you think it's a ghost?"

"I dunno, Weasel."

"Oh . . . well, what do you think it is?"

"I have no way of knowing," the old man replied. "Couldn't even tell you if it was a guy or a lady, should you ask me. In fewer words, Weasel, I haven't a clue. Listen, there's a pad and pen in the glovebox. Why don't you draw awhile?"

James opened the glove box. He retrieved the yellow legal pad, a ballpoint pen, and began scribbling -- not a drawing, but the beginning of a story.

Grandpa woke me up at 5 a.m. The sun wasn't even in the sky yet. We were on our way to a secret fishing spot. Something haunted this place . . . some thought it might be a ghost!

Dick began to wonder if taking his grandson along wasn't a smart idea. After all, what if they *did* see that strange, white shape arise out of the water? And what if it didn't retreat to the other side of the bank this time? What if it emerged, its form dripping, levitating toward them?

The idea of putting his grandson into danger did not make him feel the least bit good. Finally, he pushed the notion aside, knowing the chance of anything happening was slim.

Plumes of sandy gravel flung up behind the Ford's tires, reflected in the rearview mirror. An old song about country roads drifted through Dick's mind like a soft, mellow cloud. James scribbled away, adequately entertained.

***

They sat upon the old log, just long enough to comfortably seat them. The sun dawned, inking the sky with brilliant reds, yellows and oranges. The sky made James think of a jack o' lantern. He counted on his fingers how many months until Halloween, and wished it were sooner.

Dick cast his line, then set down the pole between the V of a forked stick he'd slid into the soft bank. James studied the river, waiting for the Shape. Dick brought along the pen and legal pad, just in case the boy grew bored.

An hour passed. James sighed, giving up hope on a mysterious sighting. He grabbed the pen and paper and began to doodle. He could think of nothing worthy to add to his story.

Dick reeled in his line, re-cast, then caught a fish. The small-mouth bass squirmed in his hand. James asked if he could touch the fish.

"Sure you can, Weasel," Dick replied, and let him pet the fish's head. "Okay. I'm sure he appreciates that, but I'm going to return him home now."

James nodded. Dick tossed the fish. It floated near the surface a moment, then dipped down and away into the brown-green water.

The sun climbed higher into the sky.

"Grandpa?"

"Hmm?"

"Can we go home soon? I'm hungry."

"Sure, Weasel. I'm famished, myself."

"What's *famished?*"

"It means really, really hungry."

Dick reeled in the line, grabbed the tackle box, then . . . froze at the sound.

Plink. Plink. Plink.

"Grandpa," James gasped. "Look!"

Dick looked. There it was. The same, vague white shape he'd seen the week before, emerging slowly out of the water. He looked from the Shape to his grandson (whose mouth hung open), then back to the Shape.

"Hello there, Mr. Shape!" James shouted gleefully.

Dick dropped the tackle box. The latch popped open, sending bobbers, lures, and hooks spilling out onto the bank. "*Shhhh, boy!*" he said.

The Shape turned just as it had done before. Its dripping form levitated above the water, floated above the opposite bank, then glided beyond the trees.

"Quick, Grandpa!" His grandson waded into the river, the stream slow and easy.

"Weasel! Get back here."

"C'mon," the boy called over his shoulder. "Before he gets away."

"Let it go, boy!"

James paid no mind, sloshing through the river until it grew deep, then swam the rest of the way. "Damn," Dick muttered, and waded into the river. His virile arms managed to carry him across, despite his boots weighing him down. Climbing onto the opposite bank, drenched and cold, he looked up in time to glimpse the back of James' jacket as he disappeared into the forest.

"*Damn!*" Dick sprinted after the boy. His sopping jeans and shirt clung tight to his skin. A wind brought goosebumps and ruffled his feather-soft, grey hair. His boots made squishing noises as he chased James deep into the forest. The odor of pine, birch, and fresh air was strong enough to sting his nostrils

"C'mon, Grandpa," James shouted somewhere ahead.

***

Branches scratched his cheeks. Burs stuck stubbornly to his pant legs. The boy was fast. So was the Shape, apparently.

There was no trail. Dodging trees became an art which the old man had yet to master. He banged his side against the trunk of a birch tree, knocking the wind out of him. After a moment, he redoubled his efforts and ran.

A steady incline made the chase exceedingly difficult. The forest floor lifted gradually, until Dick found himself climbing a steep hill, grabbing onto random trees so as not to slip and fall. His heart pounded. He gazed upward. The boy disappeared over the hill.

"Too old for this shit," Dick gasped. At the top of the hill, he paused, resting against a tree. James stood before the mouth of a cave burrowed into a tall cliff, peering into the darkness.

"Weasel," he said, trying to catch his breath. "Get . . . Over . . . Here. *Now.*"

James retreated from the mouth of the cave.

"You okay, Grandpa?"

"No, I'm not okay. Why didn't you listen?"

"I'm sorry," the boy replied solemnly.

"It's a little late for that now, I think."

The boy turned toward the cave and pointed. "That's where it went. It didn't even have *legs*, Grandpa. The Shape, I mean. It just floated over everything, right into the cave! That must be where he lives."

"Perhaps," Dick said, his pulse steadying. "But where the Shape lives is none of our business."

The Shape. A strange moniker, fitting for a strange creature. He couldn't remember if he'd come up with it, or if the boy had. Either way, it didn't matter. They needed to get the heck out of the forest and let the Shape get on with . . . whatever things the Shape did.

"Grandpa, look what I brought." James pulled a mini flashlight out of his jacket pocket. Clicked it on. The beam momentarily blinded Dick's sight.

"Put that away!" he said, squinting his eyes.

"Oops, sorry." James winced. "But we can use this to explore the cave. We can find out how it lives."

"We've already interrupted its bath," Dick replied. "Haven't we disturbed it enough?"

James shone the flashlight into the dark hollow, walking over to it.

"Get back here, boy, or I'll tell your momma."

Darkness swallowed the boy. "C'mon, Grandpa!" James' voice echoed.

Dick heaved a sigh, wiped the sweat from his forehead, and entered the cave. James stood inside, shining his flashlight into the depths. The air smelled dank and earthy. Water trickled from the walls. The floor was moist, black dirt.

"Haven't your folks taught you to listen?" Dick asked, joining the boy's side.

"They taught me to always follow my curiosity." The boy shrugged.

"Yeah, well, have you heard what curiosity did to the cat?"

"Yep," James nodded. "The cat got killed. But I'm not a cat, remember? I'm a weasel."

The old man chuckled, although his irritation was palpable. The boy simply wouldn't listen. Now they were inside a dark cave, heading in deeper by the minute.

Dick's thoughts turned to the creature. When they inevitably discovered the Shape hiding away in its home, would it become aggressive? Would it smother them with its slick, white body, absorbing them into itself like in *Invasion of the Body Snatchers*?

The thing could levitate, after all, Dick figured. *It'd be wise not to underestimate it.*

"We need to make a deal, kiddo," Dick announced. "We'll continue walking for two minutes, maximum. Then we turn around and go home."

"Okay, Grandpa."

"We have a deal?"

James nodded.

"That means when I say 'let's go', you listen, and we go. Promise?"

"I promise."

They continued onward. The darkness was silent, except for the rhythmic drip of ground water splashing from the cavern ceiling onto the floor. James pointed the electric torch straight ahead, swinging occasionally to the left, then right. Something shiny caught under the bright, yellow beam.

"Gramps, look!" James reached down and picked it up.

"Empty bottle of Miller Lite," Dick noted. "Very nice. Can we go now?"

"Has it been two minutes already?"

"Probably not, but close enough."

"One more minute, Grandpa. Please?"

"Fine. But once those sixty seconds are up, we're turning back.

"How will you know it's been sixty seconds?"

"I'll count in my head."

"How can you count and talk at the same time?"

"I can't, boy, so keep quiet."

James tossed the empty bottle aside. It clinked dully upon the ground.

"Maybe the bottle is a clue of some sort," the boy remarked as they came upon another beer bottle, this one smashed. Fragments of glass sparkled under the beam.

"Why so many bottles?" James asked.

"Probably from people throwing parties in here," Dick replied. "Teenagers, likely. They do that sort of---"

"Whoa!" James cried suddenly, directing the flashlight ahead of them.

A strange pattern set out upon the cavern floor. The pattern was made out of various rocks, strategically arranged into the shape of a star. James bent onto his haunches to inspect it. Dick frowned and bit the left side of his lip, contemplating the structure.

"Grandpa! I know what this thing is. It was in the movie, *Night of the Demons*. It's a pentagram, used to summon evil spirits!"

Dick was wary of his grandson watching so many gory movies, but at least it had added to his education, in a twisted sort of way. *The boy's right. Not a star. A pentagram.*

Next to the pentagram, more bottles of beer, and what appeared to be the dirty, shredded remains of somebody's clothes. Most of the rocks composing the pentagram matched the interior geology of the cave, yet some presented a color different from the cavern walls and ceiling. A dark crimson color, almost brown. The hair on the back of Dick's neck prickled.

The rocks forming the pentagram, he realized, were stained with blood.

"Your minute is up," the old man whispered. "Let's go."

The boy turned, shining the flashlight up at him.

"Get that out of my eyes!" Dick barked.

"Sorry." James stood, taking a final, appreciative look at the pentagram. He walked over to his grandfather. "Thanks for the extra minute."

"Don't mention it. Let's go home."

An obnoxious squeal, like nails on a chalkboard, resounded in the cave. James spun around with a cry, shining the flashlight past the pentagram, onto the wall not ten feet beyond it. They'd unknowingly reached the back of the cave.

Gathered along the far wall . . . dozens of them.

Dozens of Shapes. Their white bodies glistened bright beneath the beam. "My God," Dick whispered. The beam quivered across their gleaming forms. He put a hand on the boy's shoulder and squeezed.

The Shapes hovered above the ground. Their wet, slimy bodies made Dick think of the gross, outer sheen of a slug. "We're going to back away, boy," he said, quietly. "Nice and easy."

James nodded, his chest rising and falling in panicked rhythm. They backed away, one step at a time. The Shapes floated forward, keeping pace. James began to whimper.

"Shhh . . ." Dick whispered. "Everything is going to be---"

Sickening wet *plop* noises echoed inside the cave, as each Shape gained two coal-black eyes. The eyes emerged out of their white flesh, full of liquid, like tiny pools of hot tar. James gasped, the light trembling even more within his hands.

"Whatever you do," Dick muttered. "Don't. Drop. The light."

James nodded numbly. The Shapes approached with staring black eyes. When Dick and James quickened the pace of their backwards retreat, equally did the Shapes advance.

As the Shapes floated over the pentagram, James glimpsed something on the floor, just to the right. Curiosity somehow still functioning within the boy's frightened brain, he directed the beam over to the object. Both Dick and James gazed upon it; their eyes wide, their hearts thumping.

A human skeleton. The skull was tilted backwards, resting against the cavern wall. The jaw hung open, as if it'd died screaming. Next to it, several more skeletons cloaked in shredded rags lined the wall.

James screamed. The Shapes, each in their turn, materialized wide, horrible mouths with sharp fangs --- dripping a viscous, black liquid. The Shapes released a collective steam-whistle shriek, mimicking the boy. Those inhuman squeals reverberated upon the cavern walls, making Dick and James' ears ring.

"Run!" Dick shouted, pulling James' sleeve. They turned and ran, the flashlight beam bobbing over the walls, ceiling, and floor. The Shapes followed. A cold chill washed over Dick and James' backs, as if the creatures' bodies possessed a temperature so frigid it chilled the very air.

At last! A hint of light ahead, a hope, a beacon, a lighthouse amongst a stormy sea --- a possibility that they may make it out alive. But there was no guarantee. Behind them, the Shapes let out another ear-piercing *SCREEEEEEEEEEEEEEEEEEEEEEE*

The light around the entrance grew.

They ran out into blinding sunlight. Sprinting past the plateau around the cave, they slid down the incline, crunching twigs and swishing leaves underfoot.

James slipped and fell at the bottom, burying his chin in a bed of pine needles. Dick hauled him up to his feet, and they were running again. For all he knew, the Shapes were inches behind, gliding silently above the forest floor. He dared not look over his shoulder to check. One misspent second could mean the Shapes' cruel, dripping fangs sinking into their flesh.

They hastened onward, dodging branches and weaving around trees. Just as Dick thought they'd gotten lost, the river sounded in his ears.

Locating the bank, they jumped into the river and swam for it.

Dick arrived at the shallows, hauling James by the back of his jacket up onto the bank, where the overturned tackle box and fishing pole lay. Out of breath, trembling, soaked, Dick and James stumbled, collapsing onto the bank. The boy turned aside and vomited water.

They looked across the river. Along the opposite bank, the Shapes neatly aligned in a row. Their numbers had dwindled to six or seven. Their floating, white forms throbbed in unison, as if linked into a shared heartbeat.

Blackest eyes stared back. Obsidian liquid formed into droplets at the pointed ends of their canines, then spilt onto the bank with a steaming *hisssss*.

Yet the Shapes did not approach. They did not glide across the river to devour James and his grandfather. As if the river served as a barrier they weren't allowed to cross.

James' cheeks shimmered with wetness. Dick didn't know if it was from the river or from tears, but when he looked back at the bank, the shapes were gone.

"Grandpa?" James wiped his runny nose with a soaked sleeve.

“Boy?” Dick took off his boots, poured the river out of them.

"Those teenagers you talked about, up in that cave," James started, ". . . it was *their* skeletons we saw, I think. Maybe they built that pentagram for a summoning spell. And the Shapes . . . well, they got 'em. Got the teenagers, I mean. Ate their flesh and left the bones, like piranhas."

"That's a fair theory, Weasel," Dick replied, putting his boots back on. "I'm even liable to agree with you. Now, here's one of mine: you mentioned earlier you're a weasel, and not a cat. But if you *were* of the feline persuasion, you'd have just spent all your nine lives, boy. And it may seem safe on this side of the river, but just in case, I say we get the hell out of here."

James managed a weak nod, then assisted his grandfather in collecting the spilled contents of the tackle-box. James carried the box as they ascended the incline, following the trail through the woods back to the pick-up . . . never to visit Grandpa's secret fishing spot ever again.

From that day on, Dick and his grandson made a promise: never to tell anyone what had happened. It would be their little secret.

"Best to keep this on the down low," Dick told him, his large hands on the boy's shoulders. "People will tend to think we're crazy or just making things up. Not only that, but it might inspire curious people --- such as yourself, Weasel --- to check that spot out. And we don't want anyone fooling around, winding up like those skeletons."

James agreed 'mum' was the word, but asked if he could still write a story about their adventure. "Sure, boy." Dick nodded. "Just as long as people think it's *only* a story."

As it turned out, it would be many years before James would write that story about their run-in with the Shapes. By this time, he was twenty-five years old, and blessed with a fiancé and daughter. His Grandfather passed away from a battle with stomach cancer when James turned thirteen.

Still, the boy thought of his grandfather nearly every day --- and continued thinking of him, even after having grown into a man. Just as he thought of the Shapes; their slick, white bodies, their soulless black eyes, their dripping dagger-teeth.

But, of course, all of that is only a story.

Right?

HELGA'S HELPING HANDS

South Vietnam, 1968

A platoon of twenty-seven men slogged through the humid swamp. Bernard Patterson waded waist-deep in brackish water, an M1 carbine in his hands. Eddie Driscoll, fellow soldier and good pal, led ten feet ahead. A three-quarter moon glistened upon the dark verdant of a midnight jungle.

Mosquitos swarmed the air. Bernard slapped the back of his neck, smearing himself with blood. They rounded a bend. Reaching blindly into his shirt pocket for a pack of Camels, Bernard froze. Within the scattered foliage above the eastward bank, moonlight gleamed off the helmet of a Viet Cong, hunched in the green. Eddie, oblivious to his impending death, slogged ahead.

"*Down!*" Bernard shouted. "Eddie, get the fuck *down!*"

Edward dipped low, the water rising up to his mouth. A bullet cracked through the night, skidded across the waters, swishing inches past Edward's side. Bernard aimed his rifle. Returned fire.

The VC hidden in the grass crumpled onto the bank. Fragments of brain and cranium pattered down in a soft rain. The platoon retreated behind the bend, just as fire opened from behind the trees. Little spitballs of light escaped hidden barrels, as if the jungle were alive with lethal fireflies.

Shots rang out, splitting weeds and splintering off tree trunks and whisking through the muddy water. Thanks to Bernard's steadfast attention, not a man in the platoon caught lead.

Edward's wide eyes studied Bernard's hard, stoic gaze under the moonlight.

"Christ, Bern! You saved my ass." Eddie shook his head. "I owe you one."

"Sure as hell do," Bernard grinned. "You owe me *big time.* Remember that."

Eddie nodded, heart galloping in his chest.

Once the open fire ceased and the platoon had retreated downstream, they clapped Bernard on the back. The men were fortunate to have an astute soldier like Bernard in their midst, especially since Lieutenant Manx had died less than four hours ago.

***

Modern Day

"Bernard could use more than a helping hand. In fact, he'd do well with two!"

His wife's lame joke. One she recited over the phone to friends, followed by an outburst of chortling. Bernard's response was to groan and wheel his chair into a secluded area of the house.

Marilyn's high-pitched, mousy voice carried through the walls. Bernard knew his wife's script by heart. He'd listened to it for the last decade, ever since becoming bound to the damned wheelchair. He sat in the chair, staring out his office window while Marilyn complained as if he were a doddering old senile who could no longer hear the things she said.

As if he weren't really there at all.

"Well, you know how Bernard is," she droned. "Always has some drama or other going on. He's a lot to handle, y'know."

Bernard's gnarled fingers clutched the leather armrests. The armrests were dark green, like the jungles of 'Nam. He wished he had his old Carbine back.

A lot to handle, eh? I'll give you something to handle, Marilyn, you old nag.

A muffled response on the other line. Bernard figured Marilyn was talking to Stella, his sister-in-law. He couldn't hear Stella's side of the conversation, but her tone, faint though it was, sounded derisive.

Marilyn giggled. "Oh, yes! He's losin' his hearing aids more than ever lately. Refusing to eat. Not wanting me to strap him into the stair lift. Don't get me wrong, 'Stell, I love the man. He's just too damn *proud* is all."

They'd been a happy couple, once upon a time. Those first years of marriage had been like a fairy tale. Yet, this was life. And life, as Bernard understood it, was no fairy tale.

***

It was a hot July evening. Marilyn prepared a meatloaf and corn on the cob dinner. Bernard told her he wasn't hungry, yet she insisted he eat.

Insisted. That's what Bernard hated about his wife. She was always and forever *insisting* things.

"Look at you, Bernie." She hunkered over him at the top of the landing, attempting to strap him into the stair lift. "All skin and bones. Like a skeleton!"

He pushed her jiggling, liver-spotted arms away from the strap. "Stop with the straps, for Chrissakes!" he snarled. "And if I'm a skeleton, then you're a *whale.*"

"Don't call me that." She frowned, fists resting upon her robust hips. "The strap's for your safety. Remember the last time you refused the strap?"

Bernard remembered. Marilyn had insisted on the strap, as she always did, yet that time *he* had insisted he *didn't need the god damned thing.* The mechanical whir commenced as the chair descended the mahogany steps. It moved so slowly he'd begun to contemplate what kind of mechanism worked the chair. More than halfway down the staircase, he turned in his seat and then his ass tipped over the side. Down the remaining steps he rolled, legs sprawled and arms reaching out for the bannister, yet finding no purchase.

The following week was spent in the hospital with two broken ribs and a concussion.

He looked up at her now, studying her humorless features. All those wrinkles and lines. *When did she get so ugly?*

"Yeah," he sighed. "I remember."

"Good," she nodded. "Then you won't mind if I ---"

He pushed her arms away. "I said NO. I'll sit still this time, Marilyn, god damn it! I won't budge an inch. Just let me---"

Marilyn pushed his shoulders against the chair back and grasped the strap. Gritting his teeth, he yanked the strap out of her hands and pushed her away with what small reserve of fight he had left in him.

That small reserve, as it turned out, was stronger than he anticipated.

Marilyn gasped. She tottered off the first step, crying out as her body *thump-thump-thump*ed down the steps. The moment she hit bottom, her neck audibly snapped. Her agonized cries immediately cut away.

Bernard sat in the stair lift, chest rising and falling in panicked rhythm.

"M-Marilyn?" His green eyes floated like lily pads in the watery pools of his sclera. Silence greeted him like the peal of dreadful thunder and his heart plunged.

The old staircase curved to the right before the landing. Between the bars, Bernard squinted at Marilyn's body. Her neck had twisted one-hundred-and-eighty degrees. Her sagging old turkey neck resembled a wrung dishtowel.

Bernard called her name again, knowing it was pointless.

For the first time in many long years, he wept.

A doddering old man, halfway to infirmity, sat in the lift. The safety strap dangled to the side. Bernard's tears were rivers in the valleys of his age-weary face, streaming off his chin to water his hands. His proud, old, sinful hands.

Alone, he realized, drying his cheeks. *Alone . . . because of what I've done. No one to strap me in. No one to find my hearing aids. No one to lend a helping hand.*

As his wife had said time and again, Bernard could use more than just a helping hand. In fact, he'd do well with two.

Helga Kilmer, a slim, middle-aged woman with silver hair and a kind demeanor, possessed two such hands. Bernard had never met this woman, but his wife had.

The day after Marilyn's funeral, Helga was hired on as Bernard's caretaker. This pre-arrangement, unbeknownst to Bernard, had been written in the will of his ever-concerned, loving, dead wife.

***

Bernard pushed and grunted.

Plunk!

A sigh of relief. He reached for the toilet paper, wiped, and flushed.

Helga opened the door a few inches.

"Ready?"

"M'yeah" he muttered.

She entered the small bathroom. With one hand braced under his knees, she turned him for easy transfer into the wheelchair. Her long silver locks tickled his neck. She bear-hugged his back, lifting him off the toilet and into the chair. Helga began adjusting his legs, placing them upon the footrests before he snapped.

"That's quite enough! I can handle that much, thank you. Now, get."

Helga bit her lip, resisting the impulse to stand up for herself.

"Sure, Bernard." She got out of the way.

Bernard scowled, wheeling himself out of the bathroom. Helga considered reminding the old man to wash his hands, but thought better of it. He entered his study, a room full of dusty books, a cluttered desk, and a bay window looking out onto the back yard. She paused at the doorway.

"Bernard, would you like me to---"

SLAM!

Helga studied the wood stain, her nose less than an inch away from the door. With a curse on her breath, she went downstairs to prepare dinner.

***

Tired, Bernard wheeled himself into the bedroom and gazed out the window onto the street below. The sun dipped down behind the trees. A group of kids bicycled past. He eyed their little feet pedaling at light-speed.

Muscular dystrophy. A genetic curse passed down through the generations. It was unfair. He and Marilyn had been the same age, yet she'd retained her ability to walk just fine right up until . . . well. He didn't want to think about that.

Besides, in an odd way Marilyn never really died. Helga Kilmer, although much younger than his wife, substituted for her as *World's Most Annoying Nag.*

Chrissakes, he thought. I know I can't do things like I used to, but at least I can wheel myself 'round! It's the standing and walking I can't deal with, is all. Marilyn . . . always nagging me about eating. Nagging me about washing my hands. Nagging me about what to wear and where to put my hearing aids. God, it never stopped. And now, this Helga bitch! She's like my wife's doppelganger . . .

A knock on the door.

Bernard gritted his teeth so hard he heard molars crack.

The door opened.

"I'm sorry to interrupt, but dinner is---"

"Not hungry," he said flatly.

"You have to eat."

"You have to eat!" he mimicked in a high-falsetto.

"Bernard, *please?*"

He could feel her hands on his shoulders now, caressing them.

"I'm your caregiver," Helga continued. "This is my job. If you want to live, you have to eat."

Bernard let her rub his shoulders. He had to admit it. Helga's hands felt heavenly, massaging his tired muscles. So heavenly in fact, he began to wonder what else she could do with her soft hands.

A sly grin spread across his face.

"That's the spirit, Bernard," she said. "*Now* you're relaxing. C'mon. Let's go have some dinner."

"Well, what is it?" he asked, gruffly.

"Your favorite. T-bone steak and mashed potatoes."

His stomach growled. They both heard it and looked at each other. Helga smiled faintly.

"Oh, all right," he sighed. "Get outta my way so I can get to the stairs."

Helga nodded and stepped aside. When they reached the stairs, Bernard didn't even protest the safety strap.

***

Silverware scraped and clinked on porcelain. Bernard steam-shoveled pre-cut bits of steak into his mouth, chewing with his mouth open. Helga sat on the opposite end of the table, poking at her mashed potatoes while attempting to tune out the old man's obnoxious chewing and plate-clanking.

At last, Bernard pushed his plate away and belched.

"Good?" she asked.

"It'll make a turd, I guess." He shrugged. "Now, say again how you met my wife?"

Helga smiled in warm remembrance. "I was volunteering at a blood drive for the Red Cross, about a year ago. Marilyn showed up to donate. I drew her blood. We got to talkin', exchanged numbers and just kinda hit it off from there."

Bernard scoffed. "Never did understand that."

"What?"

"Red Cross," he replied. "Takin' the blood outta your own body just to give it to some asshole you don't even know!"

"There's nothing wrong with saving people's lives, Bernard," she countered, a bit more defensively than intended.

Bernard laughed and shook his head. "Whatever you say, Helga."

His frail arms flexed as he rolled his chair away from the table and over to the stair lift. He stared back at Helga impatiently.

"Okay, okay!" she said, and rose from the table.

Once setting him down into the lift, she reached for the safety strap. Bernard clutched her wrist.

"Not this time," he said. "I'm gassy. Put that belt on and you'll squeeze the shit right outta me."

"Do you have to be so vulgar?"

"The *fuck* are you talking about?"

"Fine," Hegla said. "Have it your way."

She activated the stair lift.

Whiiiiirrrrrrrrr

Bernard rolled his eyes.

"Stop following me step by step, Helga!" he barked. "I ain't gonna fall."

"I'm just doing my job." Helga's hand hovered above his chest. If he fell, she'd catch him and push him back.

He smacked her hand away.

"Ouch!" she exclaimed, surprised at how much strength Bernard had in his arms. Probably muscle built-up from pushing his chair around all the time, she thought.

Bernard refused to buy a mechanical wheelchair, even though he could afford it. His pride had him convinced that "automated wheelchairs were for vegetables, not men." Helga held out her hand again when they were three quarters up the staircase.
Bernard slapped it away.

"Stop it!" she yelled. "I'm just trying to help."

"I don't *need* your god damn help!"

Helga bit her tongue, knowing if she didn't, she'd hurl horrible curses at him. Resiliently, she held out her hand a foot away from his chest, following beside him up each step.

"Get your fucking hand away," Bernard scowled. "Get it away or so help me I'll kill you!"

Helga chuckled. "You really are something, Bernard. You know that?"

"The fuck you mean by that?"

More than halfway up the stairs now.

"Your pride, old man. Your foolish, insufferable pride keeps you from being a good human being."

Bernard glared upward, his bottom lip trembling. Helga found his expression so absurd she failed to stifle her giggles. Bernard's eyes widened with outrage and disbelief.

The stair lift clicked into place upon the top landing. Bernard grabbed Helga's forearm, yanking her downward.

Helga yelped, nearly losing balance on the landing. Bernard forced her face close to his, his grip on her arm so tight it hurt the bone. "Say it again, Helga," he growled, with eyes cold as the Antarctic. "I dare you. I double fucking dare you."

Her heart raced. The grip on her arm was painful, and the stench of Bernard's rancid breath made her wince. Tears threatened to spill, but she held them back. She wanted to tear away from him and run out of the house. No amount of money from Marilyn's estate was worth this much hassle and pain. How that woman had put up with this foul old man for so many years was beyond comprehension.

Taking deep breaths, Helga stared back into his ugly face.

"No problem, Bernard," she said. "I'll gladly repeat it for you. I said, your foolish pride keeps you from being a good human being. Have you got it *now?*"

Bernard's sneer transformed into a grin, revealing three large gaps.

"I got it all right, Helga," he replied. "And now you, too, have got it."

Locking his long, gangly arms around her waist, he viciously pulled downward. Helga screamed, reached for the banister and missed. She tumbled, flesh thudding heavily against the boards until she lay flat on her back at the bottom.

Blood poured from her gashed forehead.

Bernard leaned over the arm of the lift for a closer look.

"Stairs are a bitch, aren't they?" he laughed.

Suddenly, his gap-tooth smile collapsed into a frown. Helga's chest gently rose and fell. He hadn't expected her to survive the fall . . . especially after seeing Marilyn's twisted, broken neck at the bottom of those very stairs.

He scratched his chin with trembling fingers, wondering what the hell to do. Helga would eventually wake up and call the police. Then off he'd go to prison, convicted for murder. As a man of seventy-nine years, that isn't how he wanted to go out. Spending his golden years locked up in a cage seemed utterly undignified. What on earth would people say?

Pride raged and writhed within Bernard's black heart.

***

Brrrriiiiing.

Brrrriiiiing.

Edward Driscoll paused the season finale of *Stranger Things* and picked up the phone.

"Y'ello?"

"Eddie . . ."

"That you, Bern?

"Bet your ass it is. Remember that favor you owe me?"

"'Course I do, Bernie ol' pal," Edward said, then thought a moment. "You okay? You sound short of breath."

"Never mind that, just get on over to my house. Pronto."

Clanking down the footrest of his Lay-Z-Boy, Edward stood.

"I'll be right over to help."

"I don't need your *help,* god damn it!" Bernard barked.

Edward flinched, jerking the phone away from his ear.

"I don't need your help," Bernard repeated, calmly. "I just need you . . . to do me the favor you *said* you'd do. This is a deal, not charity. All right?"

"Sure, Bern. I'll be on over."

"You're a good man, Eddie."

Click.

***

"*The fuck?!*"

Edward's voice carried upstairs. Bernard lay flat on his stomach in his office, an old rotary dial telephone by his side. He'd barely managed to reach up and snatch it off his desk.

"Up here!" he shouted.

Edward sprinted up the stairs, then froze in the office doorway.

"Grab my wheelchair, Eddie. It's by the stairs. Tried to lift myself into it, and couldn't."

"What's with the woman on the floor downstairs?'

"Get my chair, god damn it, and I'll tell you!"

Edward carried up the chair. Although he was no spring chicken himself, he managed to scoop Bernard off the carpet and into the chair.

"You okay?" Edward asked, gripping Bernard's shoulder.

Bernard caught his breath. "No, Eddie. Nothing is 'okay'. That bitch at the bottom of the stairs? *I* did that."

Edward's brows pinched. "How, Bern?"

"I pushed her, dummy." Bernard rolled his eyes. "Thought she'd break her neck, but she's still breathing. I was on the stair lift when I pushed her. Had to crawl in here on my hands, like back in 'Nam, just to get to the damn phone."

"Jesus Christ." Edward shook his head. "*Now* what do we do?"

"Now, Eddie, you are to go down there, kill the bitch, and dispose of the body."

Crickets chirruped in the yard outside, leaves stirred in gentle breeze, yet all the rest of the world seemed to grow dread quiet.

Edward inhaled a shaky breath. "You want me to *murder* that woman?"

"You need hearing aids?" Bernard countered.

Edward paced the office. "I know you saved my life back in 'Nam and all, but I can't just kill somebody in cold blood. That's just . . . wrong!"

Bernard scowled, his green eyes resembling frozen, chipped emeralds.

"You're full of shit, Eddie," he gritted. "Remember all those gooks we killed in the war? Remember how many young, slit-eyed men died at the end of our carbines? *Do you?*"

Edward ceased pacing. "Yeah," he nodded, frowning down at the floor. "I remember."

"Good," Bernard smiled. "Then one more murder ain't gonna make you any less of a sinner. You *owe* me this, Eddie. You wouldn't be alive if it wasn't for me, remember? Now, you're going to return the favor. You're gonna save my god-damned miserable rotten life. Got it?"

"Okay, old pal." Edward sighed, almost too quiet for Bernard to hear. "How should I do this?"

Bernard grinned poisonously.

***

Sweat beaded Edward's forehead as he crammed Helga's bloody severed limbs into a duffel bag, then dumped the bag into a fresh hole he'd dug in Bernard's backyard. Chopping up Helga's body with Bernard's dull machete had taken damn near an hour. His arms ached, his head throbbed, and his back was absolutely killing him.

"Come on, come on!" Bernard shout-whispered from the windowsill, directly above the interred flower bed. Edward peered up at Bernard's ancient face in the moonlight.

"Shut up," Edward replied, long past civility. "I'm working fast as I can."

He packed Helga's decapitated head between the jangle of arms, legs, and torso. The bag could barely contain her. After zipping the bulging lid, Edward began shoveling dirt into the hole.

"Wait!" Bernard whispered.

Edward dropped the shovel, setting his gore-stained hands on his hips. "What now!?"

Grinning wide, Bernard said, "You forgot a couple pieces!"

Edward looked where he was pointing. Helga's hands lay palms up on the dewy grass, severed at the wrists.

"Ahh, shit." Edward picked them up. They were soft and cold to the touch. The zipper groaned as he reopened the bag, smashing Helga's hands into the blood-soaked limbs, attempting to make them fit.

No room. He looked plaintively up toward the window.

"Ahh, hell." Bernard chuckled, waving a hand. "Just throw 'em in the hole and call it done."

Edward didn't argue, chucking them into the space around the bag. Once having filled in the hole and patting the soil flat, he gazed upward for Bernard's seal of approval.

Bernard's head slumped. A thin strand of drool hung from the corner of his lips. Faint snores sounded from the window.

Edward returned the shovel to the tool shed. After cleaning up the bottom stairs and the bloody bathtub where he'd hacked up Helga's body, he drove home, took a hot shower, then got exceedingly drunk.

Normally he'd pass out and sleep like the dead. Instead, he'd spent the night tossing and turning with guilty nightmares.

WHACK! WHACK! WHACK!

The dreadful noise of the machete cleaving flesh. Helga's eyes had opened wide upon the first strike, closing forever with the second.

The most terrifying aspect of this dream, however, were the hands.

Helga's bloody severed hands, scooping in the soil, helping Edward fill up the hole. He'd peer up at Bernard's dark silhouette in the window, seeing only a yellow, gap-filled grin. The dream repeated itself over and over until sunlight streamed through his bedroom window. Edward awoke with the worst headache of his life and considered two options:

Grab some aspirin from the medicine cabinet . . . or grab his service rifle out of the closet, load it, and insert the barrel into his mouth.

***

Bernard's own snoring woke him. He yawned and stretched, smiling contentedly. He'd slept like a baby.

A cool breeze blowing through the open window made him shiver. Gazing down at the flowerbed, he eyed Helga's final resting place and frowned.

Edward had done a shitty job filling in the hole. There was a pronounced dip in the grave. Loose dirt scattered the surrounding grass.

Bernard wondered if some critter had arrived in the night, digging for carrion.

Or, perhaps, something had attempted digging itself out *of the grave.*

Cold dread crept up inside Bernard's stomach. He rubbed his temples. *Don't be paranoid, you old fool. It's not like Helga could get any deader. 'Specially the way Eddie did her.*

He reached up and shut the window.

D-d-d-d-drum. D-d-d-d-drum.

D-d-d-d-drum. D-d-d-d-drum.

Bernard's eyes widened. He wheeled himself around to see where the noise was coming from. A terrible chill shot up his spine when he saw it.

Not 'it', but *them.*

Helga's hands had mounted Bernard's desk, the wrists caked with dark blood. Splintered bone jutted from the stubs. All ten fingers drummed methodically upon his desk.

Bernard's heart galloped, threatening to burst from his chest. Closing his eyes, he prayed when he opened them the hands would disappear. *Nothing more than a hallucination.*

But the hands remained. The drumming fingers resounded loud as a kettle drum. Bernard put his hands over his ears.

D-d-d-d-drum. D-d-d-d-drum.

"H-Helga? Please don't hurt me. I-I didn't mean anything by pushing you down those stairs! Y-you just wouldn't leave me be is all. I'm a *man*, you know. I n-need my in-in-independence. My autonomy. Oh god, *please!* You understand don't you, Helga? Don't you?"

The fingers ceased drumming. One hand remained poised upon its fingertips, the other lifted its index finger, lowered it, then it raised again.

Bernard smiled nervously. "S-so you *do* understand. Oh! Thank God in His Divine Mercy. I'm so *sorry*, Helga."

The index finger lowered, then raised.

***

The hands did everything Helga would have done, had she lived. The hands cooked Bernard's meals. Washed his clothes. Lifted him on and off the toilet, as well as the stair lift.

It was a wonder to Bernard how the hands could do these things without the muscular mobility of arms and shoulders. It was a wonder to him how the hands could exist at all. The fact the hands couldn't complain, nag, or bitch was an additional benefit. He even grew to tolerate them, until . . . *the dreams*.

Bernard began to dream of Helga's other body parts. The ones he'd ordered Edward to shove into the duffel bag and bury in his garden. He dreamed about the bag twitching and writhing beneath the dirt, the legs and arms tussling about like thick, virile snakes in a mating dance.

Then, of course, there was the matter of Helga's head. That grey, rotting head with maggots burrowing into the flesh of its cheeks and its milky white eyes staring into the dark, the mouth opening, speaking in a low, dreadful croak: *I just wanted to help you, Bernard. I just wanted to heellllp!*

Bernard would bolt upright in bed, drenched in sweat, screaming at the top of his lungs with Helga's teeth still clattering in his ears.

This happened not just every night, but every time he dared close his eyes. He couldn't sleep at all. The nightmare replayed on an infinite loop.

Two weeks after Helga's hands first appeared on his desk, Bernard found himself staring up at his bedroom's white stucco ceiling. His heart palpitated in a slow thrum. He felt incredibly weak, and tired. More tired than ever. He knew what would happen if he closed his eyes.

Helga's dissected corpse . . . writhing, twitching, the mouth opening to speak. Even now, lying under the blankets with purple bags under his eyes, he could hear Helga's voice.

I just wanted to help . . . Bernard.

Just wanted to help youuuu.

His waking life had become a nightmare. Now, it seemed there was only one thing left to do. For the first time in all his seventy-two years, Bernard Patterson asked not for a returned favor, nor a job owed, but for honest and genuine help.

"Please, Helga!" he sobbed. "Please, just . . . just do it! Do it now. *Help me.*"

Fingers *tap-tap-tapped* down the dark hallway. Helga's hands entered the room and pulled themselves up the foot of the bed. Like two horribly big spiders, the hands creep-crawled across the blankets. Bernard felt a cold scuttling upon his shirtless chest. They were dreadfully cold and damp, their icy flesh decomposing into a dark green and stinking of dirt and rot.

Flies buzzed around the blood-congealed wrists. Fingers drummed upon his collar bone, awaiting further orders.

Bernard whimpered pathetically, then nodded. He couldn't withstand the suffering anymore. All those long, sleepless days and nights, obsessing about Helga's decapitated head and her limbs --- *oh god, those dreadful, re-animated limbs!*

Helga's helping hands curled around his throat. Yellowed cuticles cut into the flesh of his neck. Bernard's rheumy eyes bulged as his windpipe was crushed.

A dry clicking in the back of his throat.

The sound of Bernard swallowing his pride.

THE THING IN GREGORY THORNTON'S BASEMENT

Gregory Thornton was a loser. At the ripe age of thirty-two, he had just moved out of his momma's and into a decrepit two-story farmhouse with a basement. Momma bought it for him. Most would have regarded the farmhouse as condemned. Others, a fixer-upper.

For Gregory, it was simply good-as-is.

Half the roof shingles were missing, long broken and blown away by stormy nights. Puffy yellowed wallpaper complimented dirty, spider-cracked windows. Due to rain exposure, the musty floorboards were unsafe to walk in certain areas. It was home to Gregory nonetheless. He figured himself a bird who'd at last flown the nest to lay a few eggs of his own.

Perhaps that's stretchin' it, he thought, collecting the remaining O's at the bottom of the Chef Boyardee can. "Out of the can, into the man." He chuckled lonesomely.

Looking around the grimy kitchen for a place to toss the can, he realized he'd forgotten to bring a garbage receptacle. *Oh, well.* He opened the white, paint-chipped door to the basement, adjacent to the kitchen. A draft of moist earth invaded his nostrils. He fumbled for a light switch upon the wall, then for a string to an overhead bulb, finding neither. It was dark as the other side of the moon down in that basement. He chucked the can. It clanked upon the stairs, hitting bottom with a dull thud and rolling away somewhere.

Good 'nuff. I'll buy a garbage bin next time me and Momma are in town.

When that would be, Gregory didn't know. His new house was fifteen miles away from the nearest town, a shit-kick little blimp on the Kansas state map called Barnboard. He didn't own a car, so driving to the supermarket was out of the question. Gregory didn't mind not having his own transportation. After all, Momma had it covered. She always did.

Belly rumbling, he satiated his hunger with a banana, then tossed the peel down the dark basement stairs. He chased the banana with a Budweiser, then chased the already browning, stinking peel with the crushed empty can.

He enjoyed the rhythmic *clank-clank-clank* on its way down.

***

Momma picked him up in her Oldsmobile for a trip into Barnboard.

"Momma sure misses you," she said.

Using Momma's weekly $40 allowance, he purchased necessities: milk and Captain Crunch, a dozen cans of Spaghetti O's, double-stuffed

Oreos, four jumbo bags of gummy worms, and a twenty-four pack of Budweiser. He spent the remaining allowance on a Hustler magazine. He hid it from Momma as best he could, but she knew --- somehow, she always knew.

Momma gave him a big ol' kiss before he exited the car, which stunk of the compartment ashtray's detritus of smoldering, yellowed cigarettes. After ambling into the house, he chewed on gummy worms until his jaw ached, then remembered he'd forgotten to buy a garbage bin.

Opening the basement door, he dropped the empty gummy package. It floated like a feather, swallowed by the darkness. It landed upon the bottom step, the crinkle of plastic barely audible. However, he *did* hear the rattle of a can.

Rats. There's rats in my basement. Yuck! He slammed the door. Just as long as the rats stayed down there and left him alone, all would be fine.

Don't really need a garbage bin anyway.

***

Gregory licked the spoon clean of tomato sauce, then tossed the can into the basement. *Clang-clang-clang-clang, thud!* Then a wavering, metallic roll down whatever uneven slope existed down there in the dark. He sauntered onto the front porch. Sat upon the step. It was night.

Prairie field surrounded the house on all sides. Crickets cozied within tall grass sang, *rheee-rheee.*

Momma once told him it was the sound crickets made when they wanted to mate. *Rheee-reee.* Let's do it! *Rheee-reee.* Be fruitful and multiply! *Rheee-reee.*

Thinking about sexed-up insects put Gregory into one of his moods. He went inside and stooped over the centerfold of a curvy brunette with long legs splayed wider than a bear trap and did his thing all over it. After wiping the glossy page as best he could, he set it out to dry. Too many gummies sickened his stomach and he went to bed on the air mattress Momma bought him.

Gregory dreamed of the centerfold brunette, only she was different in the dream. Her legs were green, leathery husks. She smiled, mush-mouthed with wet, half-chewed gummy worms writhing on their own volition. Her long, alien legs twitched. She sung in a low, insect hum:

rheee-rheee, rheee-rheee.

They made love, her noises buzzing in his ears.

***

Momma dropped by the house one afternoon, her plump egg-shaped form barging through the doorway. Gregory had put away the

Hustler only moments before. She acted like she owned the place, because she did.

"I've got your rent all done and paid," she smiled, plump cheeks dimpling. "Ain't your momma sweet?"

"Yes, Momma. Thank you."

"You're welcome, Gregory-pegory. How's things?"

"Pretty good. Just been busy."

"Oh? Doing what?" She cocked her head like a Labrador.

"Watchin' TV, mainly," he replied. "Listening to the radio, sometimes."

"Sounds fine, sugarbumpkins. Momma just wanted to check up on you. It must get awful lonesome out here." She stuck out her bottom lip in a *'my poor baby'* face.

"I like being lonesome, Momma," he said.

"Well, ain't nothing wrong with solitude," she nodded. "Gimme a call if you need anythin', pumpkin. Love you!"

She leaned over and planted one of her sloppy kisses on Gregory's cheek, then waddled out to the Oldsmobile. She huffed and puffed, attempting to squeeze her rotund hindquarters into the driver's seat. Once situated, she flashed Gregory her pearl-white dentures and pulled out of the gravel drive. Dust clouds flew up behind her tires, then settled.

A wind blew, rattling the cockeyed rain gutter. Maybe he'd tell Momma to have somebody come fix it. He wasn't great with fixing things and entertained no delusions to the contrary.

He went inside to gorge on a bowl of Captain Crunch and watch a rerun of *Sesame Street.*

***

Months passed. Gregory paced the rooms of the first and second floor. What he'd ever do with so many dusty, barren rooms, he didn't know.

Often he found himself eating just to have something to do (after consulting Hustler, of course). During a single afternoon, Gregory devoured three cans of Spaghetti O's --- maintaining the ritual, he tossed the emptied containers down the basement stairs.

A rotten stench drifted up out of the darkness. He winced at the smell, even swooned. The cans he'd tossed had *clang-clang-clanged* to the bottom as always. Only this time . . .

A low, agonized groan rose up out of the darkness. Hairs on the back of his neck and arms stood straight.

Movement. Something rattling all those crusty, unrinsed Chef Boyardee cans. Whatever was down there didn't sound happy.

Wounded animal or something, Gregory thought, fanning the air. *Ahh, well. It can lick the inside of those cans and slice its tongue on jagged aluminum for all I care. It's got no business bein' down there, anyway.*

He leaned over the stairs, hands clutching the door frame, and shouted, "Die quietly, stupid!" He slammed the door shut. Cans clinked. Plastic crinkled. Another groan carried up the stairs. Gregory shivered.

He sat at the table, polishing off his supply of Oreos. They always helped him feel better. Once finished, he tossed the plastic tray and its shiny wrapper down the stairs, plus some empty beer cans.

***

He could hear it down there at night. It gave him the creeps. He'd lie on the flat air mattress (flat, because he'd been fooling around with matches, inadvertently burning a hole through the plastic), and listen to the thing toss around cans, crinkle wrappers, then groan.

Whether the groans were of agony or ecstasy, he couldn't be sure. It arose in a wet buzz, as if out of the throat of some mucous-congested animal. The noise always took him by surprise, even though it came like clockwork --- sounding upon every hour like some dreadful bell. A noise to make his ears twitch and his forehead grow prickly hot with fear. A noise to seal his hands in prayer.

Gregory didn't appreciate whatever was down there in his garbage disposal room.

No, Sir. Not one bit.

***

One evening, Momma arrived wearing a knee-length blue dress with yellow daisies printed on it. The thick mascara around her eyes and the smeared red lipstick reminded Gregory of a pug with its face painted. He kept this observation to himself.

"You look pretty Momma. What's the occasion?"

"Two occasions, actually," she smiled. "One's for you, and one's for me."

She held something behind her back. Then she brought it out front, shoving it into Gregory's arms. A cardboard box with five holes in the top and a twine handle. Something moved around inside.

"Go on," she said. "Open it."

Gregory opened it. Frowned.

A white, fluffy cat with emerald eyes peered up at him. He set down the box. The cat leapt out, dragging its prodigious whiskers along the linoleum, inspecting the kitchen corners.

Momma giggled. "Well, Gregory-peggory, do you like him?"

"I guess." He shrugged. *What good would a cat do me? I'd rather Momma had bought me HBO.*

"Well, he'll grow on ya," she said with a wink. "Just make sure you feed him every morning and night, and keep his water dish full."

A tall, gangly man entered the house. Standing behind Momma, he carried a bag of Kitty Deluxe, plus a cat bed, two small dishes and a crocheted catnip ball. Momma kissed the man on his lips and said, "Gregory, this is Philip. Philip, this is Gregory."

The man set down his armful of items and held out his hand. Gregory shook it reluctantly. The hand felt like moist sausage covered with tissue paper.

"Nice to meet you, Gregory," he smiled, exposing his few remaining teeth. Gregory wondered why he didn't get dentures, like Momma.

"You my new daddy?" Gregory asked.

Philip guffawed and slapped him hard on the back. Gregory's jaw clenched. Momma laughed in a high, rollicking tenor and said, "Enjoy your new kitty, honey muffin. Philip and I are off to our date. Ta Ta!"

"Ta Ta," Gregory muttered, and they were gone.

The cat weaved figure-eights around Gregory's ankles. Its white fur was soft. Maybe the cat wouldn't be so bad after all. He didn't like

Philip so much though. His breath stank and he gave a bad handshake.

Gregory's real daddy, before he'd went out for a pack of cigarettes and never returned, had been handsome. But Momma had wanted to baby him. Daddy didn't like that and left. So, Momma babied Gregory instead, and being the man of the house, he knew it was better to be babied than to just up and leave and never come back.

In the far back his mind, within a floating phantom feeling, Gregory understood all those years of dependency had left him crippled. Institutionalized.

He couldn’t imagine a life doing things for his own self.

***

That night around ten o’clock, Gregory sat at the kitchen table, snacking on gummy worms and Cap’n Crunch. He gulped three cans of Budweiser, despite his bloated stomach grumbling in protest. As the crickets outside sang their mating tune (*rhee-rhee*), he began to wonder if Momma and Phillip were fucking right about then.

He imagined Momma's cellulite jiggling and bouncing on top of Philip's reed-like figure. He attempted thinking of other things.

Large, black spiders.

The grime on the floor.

The cat's obnoxious meowing.

Momma's sagging breasts suckled by Philip's toothless maw as he arched his liver spotted back, moaning. The images persisted, bombarding his mind with various depictions of their revolting coitus.

A low, wet groan from the basement put a knot in that chain of thought, as well as one in his stomach. Cans down there rattled. It slunk around the bottom of the stairs, whatever it was. The cat, whom he'd named Binksy, brushed against the basement door. It meowed incessantly for food and water. Gregory had been too lazy to fill its dishes. He picked up the cans and plastic wrappers and shoved the cat out of the way with his foot.

He opened the door and the stench hit him full-blast; an odor comparable to the rotting flesh of a thousand animals gutted and left to fry in the sun. The trash dropped from his hands. It went clink-clanking down the stairs. Gregory swooned, falling onto his back, his legs dangling over the first few steps.

Binksy walked over the hump of Gregory's fat belly, disappearing into the basement. He raised his head to call the damn thing back, but his eyes closed before he could utter a word.

***

Midnight. He awoke to a knock at the door. Momma poked her head in. "Hellloo? Gregory, are ya still awake, honeybun?" Her slurred words were punctuated by hiccups. Philip chuckled, his hand resting upon her hefty left buttock.

"Pee-U! What's that *smell?*" she exclaimed, stumbling into the house. Then she saw Gregory lying on the floor and screamed. Philip dropped his hand from Momma's buttock, his face grown pale.

Gregory squinted in the light, his brain discombobulated with sleep and screams.

"What the hell, Momma? What's wrong?"

She dropped to her knees, wringing her hands. "What have you done to the kitty, Gregory? What have you done?!"

She sobbed. Philip's bottom lip quivered, his eyes bulging. Gregory noticed something warm and wet in his arms and looked down.

Cat remains hung limp in his arms. Its bones had been picked clean, all except for the head. A dull, lifeless sheen glazed its emerald eyes. Gregory cried out, tossing the carcass through the open basement door. The bones clattered and snapped upon the steps. Momma's shoulders hitched. Gregory stood and gazed down at his Batman t-shirt. It was soaked with blood and covered with hair and bits of intestine, the fabric sticking to his belly.

"I-I didn't do it!" he said, turning to Momma. "It was that damned thing down there in the basement."

Philip's thin face now flushed scarlet.

"You evil little shithead!" he snarled, crossing the room and throwing the first punch before Gregory even knew it. Hot pain exploded in his nose, knocking him down. Blood dribbled down Gregory's lips and chin. He staggered to his feet.

Momma, still on her knees, reached for her date's leg in an attempt to restrain him. But it was too late. Philip launched a second hard fist, this time into Gregory's stomach.

Big mistake.

The impact triggered an exodus of half-digested spaghetti O's and beer --- splattering Philip's face with tomato-red projectile vomit. The gaunt man shrieked in revulsion, holding out his dripping hands, stumbling backward. He stood in the basement doorway now, gazing down at his soiled clothes.

Gregory bolted forward, planting his right foot into Philip's crotch. Philip tumbled down into darkness, crying out with each impact upon the steps. He hit bottom, knocking around loose cans.

Silence.

Momma rushed to the doorway, cheeks drenched in rivulets of mascara.

"Philip!" she cried. "Are you all right, baby?"

No reply, except for an explosion of grotesque sucking noises --- like a high-powered vacuum with its intake tube partially covered, producing squeaks and squelches. Gregory knew the thing down there had discovered Philip's body, and was now in the process of cleaning his bones of all flesh.

Momma brayed like a wounded hound dog. "Philip! What's going on down there? Answer me, *please!*"

Gregory wiped the blood from his nose. "Your boyfriend hit me, Momma. Look, he made me bleed and all."

She glared over her shoulder, eyes like fire. "Now's not the time, Gregory Thornton!" she hollered. "Don't you ever think about anybody but your damn self? Philip is hurting down there and it's all your fault! Make yourself useful and call the police!"

She fumbled for the basement lights. Gregory watched, knowing there weren't any. He bit into his lower lip, drawing blood. Momma's words had stung him.

The squeaks and squelches grew louder. The thing down there grunted with gluttonous pleasure, like a fat man sucking juicy meat off a chicken drummie.

Gregory sprinted forward, slamming into the middle of Momma's back. She cried out, arms flailing like propellers. She caught the door frame, then spun around with eyes widened.

"Y-you . . . tried to push me down," she trembled, her face dripping with makeup. "Just like you did Philip!"

"You yelled at me, Momma!" Gregory snapped, boiling with rage. "You never done that before. I didn't like it. I didn't like that man, neither. You're *worse* than a bad parent, Momma. You're a bitch!"

Gregory grabbed hold of her pudgy legs, and hefted. Momma reeled backward, screaming. Her fingernails clawed the walls, slicing brittle wallpaper. Ass-over-teakettle, her bloated body rolled *thump-thump-thump* down the stairs. Gregory heard her neck snap on about the third-to-last stair.

The creature groaned with delight, then continued sucking, rending meat from bone. Gregory shut the basement door and went to bed.

He fell asleep to the crickets and the vulgar noises from the basement, and dreamt again of the centerfold brunette. This time her eyes were replaced with Oreos. There was nothing left of her legs but ivory bone, as if picked clean by piranhas.

They made mad, frenzied love, her Pik-Nik stick legs locked around his back. She stunk of old garbage and rotting flesh. Gregory didn't care. He devoured her crumbling, double-stuffed eyes and came inside her.

***

Sunshine streamed through the bedroom window. Gregory stood and stretched, ready for the day. Rarely had he awakened with such enthusiasm. The night's crazed events had rejuvenated him, made him feel alive. *For the first time in my life,* he thought, *I've taken charge and done somethin' for myself.*

He strode into the kitchen to fix a bowl of Captain Crunch, then froze.

The basement door hung open. Momma and Philip's bones were stacked into a jumbled pile in front of the doorway. Within the darkness above the stairs, two yellow eyes glared.

The eyes blinked --- twin flames extinguished, then lit again.

The eyes grew closer and the creature revealed itself in the morning light. Bones clattered as it slithered through them and around the kitchen table. Gregory backed toward the front door. The serpent was the most disgusting thing he'd ever seen.

Within its jaundiced eyeballs were vertical slits, black as the basement from whence it came. The head was round, fat, and gorged with grease like a meatball. A grin stretched itself wide, revealing multiple rows of needle-teeth, each incisor six-inches long. They glinted in the sun like knives.

The body tapering from the head was thick as an anaconda, trailing through the kitchen deep into the basement. Its skin undulated and boiled; a potpourri of human flesh mixed with all the discarded plastic wrappers and aluminum. The serpent's exterior was slick and tacky, glinting with shredded aluminum, moist with Momma and Philip's flesh. White tufts of hair stuck out sporadically atop its head --- Binksy's fur.

Gregory's heart pounded. His spine became a lightning rod for powerful shivers, bolting from tailbone to brainstem. Regret and shame washed over him. He longed to call out for his Momma.

The creature spoke.

"I am . . . the conglomeration . . . of your sins." Its voice was a rattling gurgle. Black-yellow bubbles arose on its face and popped, ejaculating rancid pus. Gregory's back pressed against the door. He fumbled for the knob, never taking his eyes off the serpent.

A black tongue darted out between its writhing lips --- forked, glistening, tasting air. Gregory thought it could taste his own flesh from across the room.

"*I am borne of your sloth . . . Gregory.*" Shivers jolted up his spine at the sound of his name inside the creature's horrid mouth. "*I am borne of your gluttony. I consumed your trash. I consumed your mother and her mate. I consumed their hatreds too, and they tasted gooooood. And now, I shall consume you . . ."*

The creature swayed, enchanting Gregory with its smooth pendulum motion.

Suddenly, it shot across the kitchen, teeth gnashing like a mechanical thresher. Gregory retained enough sense to pull open the door and dash. The sun was hot on his shoulders. Waist-high grass whispered against his pants. He could hear the thing behind him, calling his name in that abhorrent, rattling gurgle.

Gregory, Gregory, Gregoryyyy . . .

He sprinted through the prairie, lungs already burning from exertion. The land was flat, destitute of shelter. Nowhere to go.

Nowhere to hide.

His sweaty skin glistened under the sun and he felt everything inside him: the endless Spaghetti O's, sugary cereal, gummies, cookies and beer he'd forced onto his digestive system over the past thirty-two years. His belly flab jostled.

A whining drone resounded from the sky. Gregory gawked upward.

A small yellow airplane zipped around the field's perimeter. In the cockpit, a woman with billowing brunette hair. Although she was high above, Gregory thought she was the woman from his Hustler centerfold --- the woman of his dreams. He waved his hands in the air and screamed.

"Help! Help me please!"

But the time it had taken to cry for help was time Gregory Thornton did not have. The serpent closed the remaining space between them, sinking needle-teeth into Gregory's skull. Its eyes rolled back, exposing two pale moons.

His flesh was shredded and stripped, every ounce of blood and sinew sucked up by the creature's lethal, dagger-toothed maw, until there was nothing left but bones.

The pilot circled the field, unable to believe what she was seeing. Peering through her aviation goggles, she swooped down to get a closer look at the grotesque display.

"Incredible," she remarked. The serpent's tail expanded across at least fifteen acres of field.

Suddenly the creature shot a hundred feet up into the air like a ballistic missile and dug its incisors into the wing of the plane. The pilot shrieked as her plane dragged downward, its engine droning loudly. The modest craft crashed into the field, exploding in a barrage of flames.

After stripping and swallowing the pilot's crisp charcoaled body, the serpent slithered its still-growing mass through the field. The dry prairie was alive with bright, spreading flames. Black smoke billowed into the sky.

Ambulance and police sirens soon blared in the distance --- music to its slimy, corroded ears. For the serpent, the menu of life seemed to be expanding indefinitely.

Gregory Thornton had merely been an appetizer.

O.O.T.W

A curvy silhouette drenched in moonlight.

I am filled with sorrow and regret watching her dress. Why did she have to come here?

She shimmies into a skirt. *An earthworm writhes on hot pavement.* She reaches between her shoulders, pinning her bra. *A Black man, on the edge of death, lynched.* She shakes back her wild curls, and *the city howls like mad wolves.*

A kiss and she leaves. I am in bed. In the dark.

Alone.

Listening to the wolves howl. Faintly, perhaps at the end of the street, the sickening wet noise of flesh shredded from bone, mingled with terrible screams.

Hers.

***

Janet never came back. I'd expected as much. She was too beautiful for this world, never mind Wesson City, crime capital of the nation. She'd inevitably catch someone's eye, and in turn, someone would catch her. I told her that. She wouldn't listen.

I see her sometimes, at least I think I do. A flash of blonde curls bouncing as she turns the corner from Gluttmore onto Harridan. I chase after, only to find the path crowded with typical bums. Trash people with ugly pasts and no future. Prostitutes with grimy faces and xylophone ribs. Arms clustered with needle tracks. Sagging tattoos. A man with yellow teeth more chipped than a glacier, shouting obscenities at no one and everyone.

Yet no Janet. There never is.

I brought a woman home from Smith's Bar one night. She wasn't beautiful like Janet. We laid in bed, listening to the screaming through the wall.

"I can't stand it," Angela sniffed, her head in the crook of my arm. "Those sounds, I can't stand them."

"They'll go away," I replied. "After a while."

"You should call the cops."

"They never come."

We lay in the dark, the odor of our intimacy merged with dank air, listening to fists pound flesh. Then the noises ceased. The crying children silenced after the man told them to shut up or they'd be next.

Next morning, an ambulance and cop cars were parked outside the complex. Three mocha-skinned children, eyes brimming with tears, were eased into the backseat of one of two cruisers, while the man --- presumably their father --- was shoved into the other wearing handcuffs. The man's right eye was swollen as a grapefruit.

Two paramedics rolled a gurney toward the ambulance. The woman under the sheet did not move. One limp arm hung out, knuckles grazed raw.

Angela snuggled beside me as we watched through the window.

"Horrible," she croaked. "You should've called the police."

"At least she put up a fight."

I walked Angela home while there was still sun. Otherwise, I told her, she'd have to spend another night. She didn't want to stay. I thought that was wise.

***

I noticed the bouncing blonde curls first. Then long legs beneath a mid-thigh indigo skirt, her strut punctuated by clicking heels. We were on Harridan Street. Men howled in the alleyways. Some of the women did too. I'd been on my way home from the bank after cashing my unemployment check. What was Janet doing here? Didn't she know she could get killed in this part of the city? It'd been a month since the night she left and I'd heard her terrible, agonized screams. It flummoxed me she was even alive.

"Janet!" I ran down the street. "It's me, Wesley! Wait!"

She turned the corner onto Hennepin. So did I. Already at the far end of the street, she gazed over her shoulder. Our eyes met. Her irises shone like dazzling emeralds.

"Wait!" I sprinted down the sidewalk.

A bum jutted out a rusty Folgers can full of pennies, rattling it in my face.

"Get away, damn it!" I batted the can away, returning my gaze to the street.

Janet was gone.

My heart galloped as I raced to the four-way intersection. The bum screamed behind me, rattling his can.

The cracked, asphalt roads were congested with traffic, red lights, pedestrians. Where'd she gone? Perhaps she'd hid in an alley way, or flagged a cab. Maybe she'd stepped into one of the ramshackle apartment buildings. Hell, maybe she'd vanquished into thin air. More and more, Janet was proving as elusive as God's love.

The window of a second story apartment directly above shattered. Glass rained down. I stepped back in the nick of time.

WHAP! A man smacked the sidewalk face-first, cracking his skull wide open. Blood pooled, then dripped into the gutter. Drivers continued honking and cursing at each other, nonplussed.

Gazing up at the broken window, a hollow-eyed man stood there, scowling with what appeared to be a small bag of cocaine in his hand.

As Mr. Rogers would've said, it was another beautiful day in the neighborhood.

***

I spent the evening with a sick curdling in my stomach. The woman I loved was out there somewhere. According to *Wesson City Tribune*, up to a dozen murders were committed every night in this city. I was fine with this, so long Janet was not among that victim tally.

I gripped the grimy doorknob of Smith's Bar and entered. Maybe I'd find Angela there and she'd come back to my apartment. She loved me, she said, and I was fine with that. Angela was no Janet, but she was a warm body to lie next to. Someone who would distract from the ringing gunshots and agonized screams of the night.

And the blood-curdling howls, of course.

Every full moon, all the psychopaths and rapists of Wesson City assembled into a maddening choir. You could hear them out there in the witching hours --- a howling emitted at such spine-tingling pitch you wanted to jam your ears with cotton and sleep with all the lights on. Like clockwork, *Wesson City Tribune* would report an overnight increase in murder count the following day.

Every full moon --- mark my words *and* your calendar.

I plopped down on a stool. Smith tended bar. He had a face not even his mother could love, all pock-marked jowls and deep, inset eyes.

"What'll it be?" A voice like gravel in a blender.

"Shot of Jack, and a Corona."

I'd just about downed the shot and beer the moment he set them down.

"Another?"

"Keep 'em coming."

The bar clock read six p.m. I was the only person in the joint, except for one barfly face-down at a corner table. Smith wiped down the bar with a grimy rag. I thought about Janet.

Love is madness. I barely knew who Janet was, but it didn't matter. The slow corkscrew twist of my heart was undeniable.

I'd met her standing in line at the bank. We'd talked about the weather while our eyes discussed the bedroom. The moment she'd spoken, I sensed she was lonely.

"Smith? Another round."

She'd wanted to come home with me. She said so in the bank. With those entrancing green eyes and plunging neckline leading to petite, adorably freckled breasts, I didn't ask questions.

Smith served my poison. I downed another shot, wetting my parched throat with the beer. Alcohol sloshed around my empty stomach.

Janet and I had made love that night. The best I'd ever had. She'd taken the Lord's name in vain a dozen times a minute. Her hips thrusted, battering my pelvis as if it were the end of the world and she'd never do it again. She got dressed after the fourth round.

"You shouldn't go."

"I do what I want." She buttoned her blouse with a cheeky smile.

"That's fair, but it's dangerous at night."

"Just because I'm a woman, doesn't mean I can't handle myself. Do you think I'm weak?"

I shook my head. "Hell, even I don't go out at night. A strict policy of mine. You should know there's . . . well, creeps out there."

"You mean crack heads and pimps? Yeah, I got that. Been raised in places like this all my life, Wes. I've learned a thing or two about how to defend myself."

"Listen, I didn't mean---"

"Shhh." She bent down and kissed me. "I'll be fine. I don't live more than a few blocks away."

"Stay for the night," I prompted. "Come on."

"I'm going home to my own bed." She winked. "G'night, tiger."

She kissed me long and passionately for the final time. Then she was gone, her screams cutting deep into the night not two minutes later. Yet we'd locked eyes today. I was sure of that.

Then came the bum, rattling his can, obscuring my vision just long enough for her to turn the corner. She may as well have disappeared into an alternate dimension.

It was clear she was avoiding me. Her company had lifted me up to lofty heavens, had exulted my spirit for a few soaring, moonlit hours. Yet when she left, she'd merely made a lonely man lonelier.

I thought of the bum and his rusted Folgers can rattling in my face. My teeth clenched. I wished he were here right now, just so I could bludgeon him to death with his own can. If not for him, I would've caught up with Janet.

Now it was just me and fat ol' Smithy, asking if I wanted another round.

"Yes," I told him. "Another and another."

Night descended. I barely noticed. The barroom door swung open. The riff-raff piled in. I shouldn't have stuck around so late. Nearly nine o'clock. But I was wasted and sick and here came the crumbs and Janet was gone, gone, gone. What did it matter?

I reminded Smith to pour another damn shot and beer. He did so. The motley men, women and gender-benders ordered drinks, played pool, lit up the jukebox with punk rock songs. Smith served at a frenzied pace, rolls of cellulite jostling beneath his baggy t-shirt as he retrieved empty bottles and poured into tiny glasses.

Someone tapped me on the shoulder. I turned.

A man with glowing, yellow eyes.

I hardly noticed the gleam of his black leather jacket, nor his white fedora, and certainly not his wing-tip shoes --- not until later, when those piercing eyes were directed elsewhere.

"What?" I mumbled, unsure if I was hallucinating.

The man with yellow eyes smiled.

"You're a lonely man," he noted, plopping down on the stool next to me. "A lonely, sad little man. Callused. Self-pitying. Angry."

"Say, you read palms too?" I replied, dryly. "Get the hell out of my face. I don't care what color your eyes are."

Yellow Eyes chuckled. "Tough guy, eh? Yeah. I know your kind. Sure 'nuff 'n yes I do, as my Granddaddy used to say. Bet I could help you feel better, though."

Liquor burned in my throat. I slammed the shot glass down.

"Sorry, pal. Nobody can make me better, except one and she ain't here. Peddle your wares somewheres else."

The man grinned like a wolf, his ivory teeth filed into sharp points. I wanted to punch them out. Wanted the warm blood of his gums on my knuckles. I gazed into his banana-slug yellow eyes. Probably only contacts, but something about them made me unclench my fists.

Yellow Eyes turned to Smith, who set down a highball of whiskey before him. He swallowed the shot unenthusiastically, as if it were cough medicine.

"You're looking for Janet," Yellow Eyes said, sliding the empty highball across the bar. "Am I right . . . Wesley?"

Glass of beer mid-way to my lips, I dropped it on the bar. It landed upright, suds sloshing over the rim. "How'd you know my name?" I demanded, the room beginning to spin. "And how do you know Janet? You trailing me?"

Yellow Eyes nodded toward the door. I looked. Immediately my heart began to fox, trot, lope and lace like a half-brained pony. The door swooshed shut behind her. I couldn't believe it. Janet strutted over, high heels tapping burnished wood.

She claimed the stool to my left. Long curls flowed over her shoulders like gold. Her eyes shimmered; eyelashes batting over two gems of preternaturally green light.

Yellow Eyes gripped my shoulder.

"Still want me to peddle my wares elsewhere, Wesley?" He spoke into my ear, his tangy breath smelling like copper. Like blood.

Janet placed a hand on my knee and smiled. Her long, slender fingers slid down my thigh and massaged my crotch, coaxing me into a groan. She leaned in, hair tickling my cheeks, providing a glorious view of her décolletage. Like Yellow Eyes, that coppery scent wafted from her satin-smooth-worth-dying-for skin and lingered in my nostrils. If they bottled her scent and sold it as perfume, they'd call it *Lust*.

Shifting from her chest to her beaming eyes, I became transfixed. I was hers. I'd do anything for her. I didn't even notice Yellow Eyes had kept his hand on my shoulder.

Her plush, red lips an inch from mine, she whispered, "I've missed you, Wesley."
I faltered for reply. "B-but every time I've seen you on the street . . . you've hidden."

"Don't take it so personal, darling." She smiled, and her lips cracked as they widened, stretching to her ears. *That,* I knew, must've been my drunken imagination. "You see," she continued. "You weren't ready, and I wasn't ready. But tonight? We'll both be ready."

"It's a very special night for all of us," Yellow Eyes added.

"What's so special about it?" I mumbled, still entranced by Janet's beaming gaze.

Yellow eyes turned me on the stool's spin-seat. His wolfish smile reappeared and his eyes glowed like two clods of gold. "See all the fine people in this bar? They work for me. They do as I tell them. Soon, you will too."

The crowd occupying every inch of the barroom suddenly stopped and stared at the three of us. All of them grinned with unnaturally bright eyes, like cats staring out from a pitch black alleyway. I noticed, for their first time, their sharp teeth . . .

Yellow eyes snapped his fingers. "Yoo-hoo! Wesley? Listen up."

Janet's hands massaged my shoulders. Out of my peripheral vision, her fingers appeared inhumanly long, each digit nearly a foot in length. I almost screamed, but Yellow Eyes fixed me with his penetrating gaze. I froze, unable to break eye contact.

"We've known about you for years now," Yellow Eyes continued, "But it's against the Order to barge people's doors down, somewhat on the same grounds vampires cannot enter your home unless invited in. You were smart enough not to come out at night. Until now."

The hair on the back of my neck prickled. Janet dug her nails deep enough into my shoulders to draw blood. I winced.

"You're one of the few mortals left in the city, Wes. After tonight, you'll be one of us. Best of all, you'll have your Janet."

"That's right, baby." Janet whispered in my ear. I shuddered.

"My advice?" Yellow Eyes smiled. "Make it easy for yourself."

He downed a final whisky shot, then cupped his hands around his mouth. "Initiation Time, gang! Grab him."

Janet shoved me. I tottered off the stool onto the floor. The haggard crowd of bums, punks, junkie prostitutes, and an assortment of freaks fit for the sideshow drug me toward the door. The heels of my sneakers squealed as I pressed them against the floor.

"Smith!" I hollered. "Smith, call the police!"

"I would," he replied from behind the bar. "But they never come."

Smith's eyes turned bright red before the door closed. I writhed within the grip of my captors, yanking to the left and right. Some punk with a pink Mohawk kicked me in the stomach. Bile rushed out of my throat, soaking my shirt with upchucked suds.

Yellow Eyes led from the front. Janet trailed behind. She watched me with that inhumanly wide grin, licking her lips. Not out of seduction this time. Out of appetite.

My every attempt at escape was met with sharp jabs to the ribs and kicks to the face. White sparks flooded my vision, reducing all to doubles before clearing again. Blood streamed from my broken nose, dripping down my lips and chin. In the dark firmament above, a full yellow moon approached its pinnacle.

I shrieked for help until my throat grew raw. Cars passed on the street, never slowing, and I thought of the man who'd been pushed out the window. How his skull cracked and bled on the sidewalk. How the city had not paused. How it kept mindlessly moving like the infernal machine that it was.

***

I was dragged into an alley, where the stench of feces and decay hung thick. I was too exhausted to fight any longer. Bums, junkies and whores clustered around me, staring down with brilliant, crazed eyes.

My back touched wet pavement strewn with garbage. Rotten banana peels. Used needles. Soiled condoms. "Bastards . . ." I moaned, shivering in the dark alley. Yellow Eyes stepped to the front of the crowd. "Angry, lonely little man," he nodded. "A perfect fit for the O.O.T.W."

"The fuck are you talking about?" I asked, trying to sit up.

"Order of the Wolf," he explained, placing a heavy boot on my chest. "These lovely creatures you see before you are angry and lonely too, Wesley. I mean, can you *imagine* how enraged and alone it makes us feel --- to see people go about their lives, unaware of how truly bestial and primordial they are? You see, here in the Order, the Beast Within is *embraced*. Accepted with a full heart. In a world gone mad, the Beast is our only salvation. An affirmation of our true nature."

"Satanist!" I managed to shout, though his foot weighed like a pile of bricks upon my chest. "That's what you are, right? A bunch of drug-addled devil worshippers!"

Yellow Eyes removed his foot, allowing me to breathe fully again. He shook his head solemnly, the wolf-grin nowhere in sight. "There are no Gods, or Devils, Wesley. There is only us. We are the Beasts of the world. And now, it is time."

"Time?" I shouted. "Time for what, for Chrissakes?"

Yellow Eyes turned away, merging with the mob. Everyone's head titled upward, phosphorescent eyes fixed at the space between the buildings. The moon inched its way into the space like a giant, yellow slug.

Janet stepped forward, ripping off her skirt and blouse, tossing them aside. There was a scar in the form of a circle, beginning just below her breasts and ending at the thatch of blonde pubic hair. Within the circle, two downward triangles locked together --- like fangs.

That scar certainly hadn't been there the night we'd made love.

Her knees scraped pavement as she straddled me. Moonlight gleamed upon off her svelte, pale body. Bending low, her erected nipples grazed my chest as her tongue swirled inside my mouth.

The mob burst into a choir of howls. I wanted to cover my ears, but my arms were trapped beneath Janet’s knees. Ear-piercing odes to the lunar sphere bombarded the night.

That was when Janet’s face began to twitch. Her cheeks, jaw, and forehead writhed, shifting into unnatural locations. Bones crackled, snapped and twisted until her face undulated like a sack of snakes. I wanted to scream, managing only dry rasps.

Janet's nose elongated into a moist snout. Coarse black hair sprouted across her face, soon covering her entire body. Her ears grew into fine, elfin points. Fingers stretched and popped, the nails hardening into sharp black claws.

The moon shed its jaundiced glow upon Yellow Eyes and his cult of howlers as they transformed. Janet dug her claws into my belly. I sucked in air through grated teeth, clutched onto her hips so hard they drew blood. The thing called Janet growled, taking pleasure in my agony.

She branded their Insignia into my chest with her sharp claws. Blood dripped from the incision of two down-facing triangles set within a wide circle. Suddenly Janet's giant maw of sharp incisors sunk into the soft flesh of my neck. I squeezed my eyes shut, crying out in excruciating pain. Hot blood cascaded down my chest and shoulders. The night smelled of tangy copper, alleyway rot, and death.

Finally, the lycanthrope mob stalked away on all fours. Janet's glowing eyes seemed to float in the air, directly above sharp teeth coated in blood.

Mine.

***

A chilly, wind-swept night. The moon is rising. Tonight will be one of Initiation. *My* initiation. I will change for the first time, just as Janet has changed, just as everyone in Wesson City will one day change.

Change into what we truly are, *on the inside.*

Yellow Eyes has now put me on Recruitment Duty. Janet teased me for a month, manipulating me into pursuing her down unknown alleys and crowded streets. Now, I am doing the same with Angela.

She left her apartment one morning, on her way to work. I stood beside her car. She gasped, dropping her stack of files on the ground. Papers scattered to the wind.

"Your eyes," was all she said. The rest was a series of stammers. I walked briskly down the street, and turned a corner. O.O.T.W. members waited beneath a manhole. They lifted the cover and I joined them, dragging the cover back into place. Angela ran past, calling my name.

Tonight, she holds my hand. "I've wanted so dearly to see you this past month," she says.

Something I already know.

Mother Moon has almost reached her pinnacle. White luminescence fills my heart with ravenous lust. I want to lunge. Want to rip open her jugular and drink from the Spring of Life.

"Where are we going, Wes?" she asks. I study her azure eyes, knowing one night they would change into something far more beautiful.

"To a party," I answer. "It'll be fun."

I'm not lying. We'll be having one *hell* of a party, all right. Just for me. Tonight, I will change into the Beast --- the One that Lurks Within. And I will take her for my first kill.

I gripped Angela's sweaty palm.

"Your eyes . . ." she repeats. The Order waits in the alley. As soon as she sees them, she reels backward, shrieking for help.

Yellow Eyes and I drag her into the alley. We throttle her into submission. Soon she lays upon the icy pavement, crying, skirt ripped up one side and lips trickling blood. I stroke her hair, telling her everything will be fine --- perfect, in fact.

Janet stands beside the rest, observing with her dark, ear-to-ear grin. Mother Moon arises in her sky-bound throne, bathing us in sacred light. Everyone shines their beaming eyes upward, howling with reverence. My jaw, cheeks, forehead, and nose contort, twisting and snapping into a new configuration. The bones and muscles within my chest and legs follow, and the pain is immensely beautiful.

My brother and sisters transform --- forming snouts, pointed ears, dagger teeth. A thick coat of fur covers our flesh. I lift my true face to the moon. Exerting all the breath within my lungs, I howl deep and sonorously into the night.

The sustained note flowing out of my mouth is primordial --- sounding across thousands of years of time and lore. I've never felt so alive. For I am one with the Glory of the Beast --- that denied power within us which aches to escape all our lives.

I inhale sweetest air through flexing nostrils. Angela's fear is as pungent as the sour urine running down her legs. Long white teeth push through my gums. I sink them deep into her freckled shoulder. Angela screams --- a sound no different than that of any other victim of urban brutality.

The bliss of her blood flows down my throat, satiating thirst. I am filled with pride, expanding my Order's lineage.

Wesson City is the capital of the Beast. Soon, there will be no mortals left walking its streets. Yellow Eyes, our pack leader, will lead us onward. The O.O.T.W shall fulfill its mission.

Our legion will increase city by city, state by state, country by country, until the world is One. Nothing can stop us. We will spread like an insidious plague, crossing the seven seas, making a mockery of mankind's superficial borders, laws, and customs.

We will huff, and we will puff, and we will blow all your doors in.

For this world belongs not to man, but to the Order of the Wolf.

AVERY'S DOG

Ollie is an ancient, foul-tempered, short-haired German pointer with a high chance of winning this year's contest for *World's Ugliest Dog*. Of course if *you* lived to be a sixty-eight year-old canine, you'd be pretty mean and gross looking too. That's sixty-eight *human* years, by the way, not doggie.

Ollie is a product of SelectBreed Incorporated, a clandestine organization specializing in "genetic excellence", or, what I tend to refer to as, "genetic tampering" in "nature's business".

Word to the wise: Do not buy an animal from SelectBreed Inc.

***

Avery's funeral was just as I'd expected --- a relief.

Getting out of the house and seeing people again proved cathartic, even if said people were crying and besotted with grief. You see, I've been cooped up in the house ever since Avery died, taking care of Ollie --- who (other than myself) had been Avery's most loyal companion.

I hung around after the funeral, guzzling countless glasses of Merlot. I may or may not have hit on a few of Avery's lady friends (his ex-coworkers, specifically). The thought of returning home to Ollie had the peculiar effect of driving me to near desperation. I tried to convince a woman (can't recall her name) to go to dinner with me. When she refused, I asked her girlfriend, then her girlfriend's girlfriend, and onward down the line. Can you believe they *all* turned down this seventy-five year old man? What is this world coming to?

Two hours fleeted by, and I drunkenly assisted in folding up chairs and storing away tables. Then I drove home, wipers slapping the rain drizzled windshield. Before entering my house on Wallace Street, I stood on the front lawn, soaking myself in cold, autumn rain. Drenched and drunk-happy, I ambled inside.

The moment I walked in the door, Ollie greeted me with a toothy snarl. Half his chocolate brown coat is missing, exposing patches of scabby pink flesh. His ribs stick out, obvious as xylophone keys. Tell the truth, sometimes I feel like grabbing a stick to see if I can strike notes.

"Good evening to you too."

A strand of drool stretched from the corner of Ollie's lips down to the floor. It just hung there, connecting his mouth with the refurbished hardwood three feet beneath his slobbery jowls. Rather impressive, I thought.

I stripped naked at the door, not wanting to leak all over the hallway on my way to the bathroom. Bundling my soaked clothes, I hauled them to the tub.

As I wrung them out, Ollie growled from the doorway.

"The hell do *you* want?"

His throaty bark sounded like a blender of broken glass and nails.

"I'll feed you in a moment. Go away."

Ollie barked. I winced, feeling the beginnings of a headache crawl into my temples and root there. I hung my socks, pants, underwear and shirt up on the shower bar. Ollie's incessant, ear-shattering din continued.

At wit's end, I spun around. "Keep quiet, you genetic defect!"

He stared at me now, mouth locked into an ear-to-ear grimace of pointy teeth. His eyes were black as tar pools. Except in the very back of his eyes, the slightest glimmer of white --- a spark in all that darkness.

Ollie, SelectBreed Inc's top of the line product back in 1953, had been a decent pet to begin with. Yet as he slowly aged, his temper regressed into nastiness. These days, his eyes conveyed a coldness which seemed to say

Better watch how you treat me. I might just leap when you least expect it, sink my teeth into your neck, and rip out your jugular. You wouldn't even have the chance to scream. So you better be good to me. Be nice, and beware.

I held up my hands, attempting a smile. Ollie's glare did not break, and my standing bare-assed naked before all those snarling teeth did not boost my confidence.

"Just kidding, Ollie," I cooed. "I'll be in the dining room with your dinner in just a moment."

The growling canine turned around, his nails clicking down the hallway. I wiped the sweat from my forehead.

After throwing on P.J.'s, I dropped two cups of *Big Bites* dogfood into Ollie's ceramic dish, then refreshed his water bowl. Ollie dropped his mug into the dish, and chowed down.

"Happy now, you grumpy bastard?" I muttered.

His hackles stiffened, and I excused myself to the kitchen. After pouring a glass of Jack Daniels, I plopped down on the living room recliner to read a book.

I tried not to think about the loss of my best friend, ol' Avy Donahue. I tried even more not to think of this newest edition to my household.

Damn you, Avery. I love you, but damn you and your will and your final wishes. You could have left me your vinyl collection of 60's psychedelia. You could have left me your Volvo. But, no. You left me your unnaturally old, decrepit, genetically-malformed dog.

Man's best friend, my ass.

***

July of 1953.

I sat on Avery's front porch beneath the sweltering sun. We'd just finished playing ball with ten other kids down at the diamond. We were drenched in sweat. Not a breeze stirred. The cold bottles of Coca-Cola from Mrs. Donahue's fridge helped a little, though not much.

"Wanna go inside and watch television?" Avery wiped his forehead for the umpteenth time. Before I could answer, Mr. Donahue rolled up the driveway in his '57 blue Chrysler convertible.

"Hello, boys!" Mr. Donahue stepped out of the car, wearing a handsome suit and a bright red tie. "Avery, have I got a surprise for you!"

Avery ran over to his old man. I stood on the porch, Coca-Cola bottle sweating in my hand.

"Is it the train set from Don's?" asked Avery.

Mr. Donahue grinned. "Even better, my boy."

How could anything possibly be better than the electric train set in the display window of Don's Department store? Every boy in the neighborhood had salivated over its golden rails and steam-powered locomotives as if they were fresh baked donuts --- including myself, of course.

Mr. Donahue opened the back passenger door, reached inside, and drug out a cardboard box. He set the box on the ground. The box shifted to the left, then right.

Avery looked up, frowning quizzically.

"Well, go ahead! Open it."

Avery opened the box. "Wow!" he said, lifting out the puppy. Its face and ears were chocolate brown, with a white body splotched with ochre spots. Avery held the dog up like a champion's trophy.

"Tim! Look what Dad got me!"

I surged with envy. No way would *my* parents buy me a puppy, even though I'd wanted a canine companion for years. On the other hand, Av looked dang happy, and that puppy was plenty cute. Reluctantly, I descended the porch steps, then scratched the dog behind its ears.

"Gee," Avery bellowed. "Thanks, Dad!"

"You're welcome, kiddo." Mr. Donahue ruffled his son's hair. "But you have to promise to take good care of him, Av. That means feeding him, making sure he has fresh water, and taking him out to potty. You'll have to do those things every day, in addition to your other chores."

"No problem, Dad. I'm going to take real good care of him. Aren't I, little buddy?" The pup licked Avery's chin, making him giggle.

"His name's Ollie," said Mr. Donahue, with a wink, "and he's a very special dog indeed. But I'll explain all that inside. It's hotter than Hades out here!"

Mr. Donahue loosened his tie. We sauntered into the cool, shadowy house. Mrs. Donahue's heels tapped on the hall's tiled floor. She kissed her husband on the mouth, then bent down to pet the puppy.

"Look what Dad got me, Mom!"

"It's from *both* your mother and I," Mr. Donahue interjected. "In fact, it was your mother's idea from the get-go."

"Gee wiz, thanks Mom!"

"You're welcome, sweetie. When the salesman called with the offer, I couldn't refuse. You like the puppy?"

"I love him," Avery answered definitively.

"Good," she smiled, turning to me. "Would you like to stay for supper, Tim? You could stick around and play with the puppy."

"Thank you, Mrs. Donahue," I nodded.

"Would you like another coke?"

"Still working on my first," I said, holding up the bottle, "but thank you, mam."

"Well, if you want another, just help yourself. Sure is hot out there!" Her brown curls bounced as she walked away into the kitchen. I followed Avery and his new puppy into the living room. Mr. Donahue plopped down in his designated recliner. He brought out a pipe from his inner jacket pocket, loading the bowl with stringy tobacco. Avery sat with his back to the silent television, watching Ollie sniff around.

"Think I can teach him high-five?" Avery asked.

"Sure," I replied. "You could teach him lots of things. I've heard it's good to start while they're still puppies."

Mr. Donahue puffed away, exuding white clouds of sweetly redolent smoke. "Avery," he said, "if the company I purchased that dog from was even *half* honest about its animals, that dog is going to grow up to be *very* smart."

"Mr. Donahue?" I said. "If you don't mind my asking, where *did* you buy Ollie?"

"Business operating out of Boston," he replied between drags. "SelectBreed Incorporated. That's the name of the place."

"Huh," I said, intrigued.

"According to SelectBreed," Mr. Donahue continued, "Ollie is supposed to be *three* times more intelligent than your average dog."

"How can they tell?"

"Dunno, exactly," he shrugged. "The CEO of SelectBreed, Mr. Gundry was his name, gave me a tour of the Boston plant today. Basically, from what I observed on the tour, the animals they're sellin' --- dogs and cats, mostly, but also hamsters, snakes, even parrots --- are bred for genes of high intelligence and long life-span."

Avery held up Ollie and said, "It's *Super-Dog!*"

Mr. Donahue laughed amiably. "Yes, something like that."

"If I'm understanding you right," I said, "Ollie here might grow up to be as old as my Grandpa?"

"Mr. Gundry claimed Ollie would even outlive *me,*" replied Mr. Donahue.

"But Dad," Avery interjected anxiously. "You're not gonna die for a long time, *right?*"

"That's right." Donahue nodded, tapping his pipe's ashes into a glass tray. "Not for many, many years yet. Although to be honest, I don't entirely believe Mr. Gundry's length-span claim. I think he was being . . . ohh, what's the word . . ."

"Hyperbolic?" I suggested.

His head darted up, smiling. "That's right, Tim. *Hyperbolic*. An exaggeration. Precisely."

Little did any of us know at the time that Ollie would outlast both Mr. and Mrs. Donahue, Avery's future wife, Caroline, my own parents, and even Avery himself.

Heck. Ollie will probably outlive me, too.

***

Something like feces mixed with rotting meat wafted under my nostrils. My eyes fluttered open, and that hot July summer in 1959 was now replaced by a decrepit dog resting its paws on my knees while I sat in my recliner. Ollie's tongue bobbed with each foul exhale.

"Gross!" I exclaimed, pushing him off.

I expected him to snarl at me. Instead, he whined, laying his head down on his front paws.

His breath might stink, and he might be a grumpy old dog, but he meant well. He was just old and, like me, long past his expiration date. I reached down, scratching him behind the ears.

"Consider a tic-tac," I told him, then went upstairs to bed.

***

The weeks passed like molasses through a sieve. I missed my old pal, Avery. So did Ollie.

Ol' Jack Daniels repeatedly came to my rescue. Ollie's emotional outlet, however, were his chicken-flavored chewies, upon which he gnawed relentlessly.

On rainy days, Ollie would whine, limping around on swollen, arthritic paws. My knees always act up on rainy days, but I'm positive my discomfort was minor compared to Ollie's.

I felt sorry for the old bastard. After all, he'd lost his best friend too. And I was surely no replacement for Avery. Not after well over sixty years of companionship. I had the feeling if Ollie knew where Av's tombstone was, he'd lay down there and howl.

Ollie and I took a walk around the neighborhood one day in mid-October. Ollie's snout traced the ground for delectable odors while my mind wandered interminably through the past, present, and future.

That's why when Ollie ceased walking and sat in the middle of the sidewalk, I stumbled, nearly tripping over him.

"God damn it!"

Ollie's tail swished across the pavement like an excited windshield wiper, brushing away fallen leaves. I followed his gaze.

There sat Avery's old, two-story house. Ollie recognized it as easily as I'd recognize my bottle of Jack. He whined, staring up at the old house with wanton, brown eyes.

"Poor boy," I said, "It's going to be all right." I reached down to pet him. Ollie launched his teeth onto my hand in one swift movement. I retracted.

"Bastard!"

Ollie ran up onto Avery's front porch, the leash dragging behind him. Blood dripped from my fingers. The skin over my knuckles had been raked, yet there were no puncture wounds. I ripped off my denim jacket, wrapping it around my hand.

Ollie clawed at Avery's door, engraving marks into the wood.

"Ollie!" I shouted.

His head swiveled around. A slim white etching, like an electric spark, glowed within the depths of his pupils. He growled, snapping at the air like a sprung mouse trap.

"Have it your way," I yelled and stalked off down the street. Before turning left onto Asimov Street, I gazed back. Ollie remained clawing at the door. I shook my head, exhaling sharply, then walked home with my jacket swaddled around my hand.

After running my stinging fingers under cold tap, I bandaged them, then spent the evening downing a fourth of J.D. at the dining table.

***

May of 1974.

The green tennis ball flew through the air. Ollie leapt, caught it, then brought it back to Caroline.

"Good boy," she said, patting Ollie's head. "Now, drop it!"

Ollie dropped it. Caroline wiped the drool and grass blades off the ball.

"Ewww!" she said, then tossed it high for Ollie to chase.

"Dinner's done," Avery announced, kissing Caroline on the lips. "Tim? Johanna? Help yourselves!"

Johanna and I loaded our plates with juicy burgers and bratwursts, then sat at the picnic table in Avery and Caroline's lush backyard. Ollie dropped the ball beside Caroline's feet, staring up at her with those charming, puppy dog eyes.

"No begging, Ollie." Caroline wagged her finger.

Ollie trotted over to my side of the table. Occasionally, I fed him bits of burger. He lapped the meat from my fingers, always gentle. Birds chirruped in the overhanging branches. I studied Johanna's smooth, tan face, dappled with leafy shadows. The burgers were fat, juicy, melting in our mouths.

"You do a fine job with that grill," I told Avery.

"Thanks, buddy," he grinned. "Say, you're not feeding Ollie, are you? We're trying to break that habit."

"You kidding?" I said. "No way is Ollie getting any of *my* food. It's too damn good." Avery nodded and gave me a thumbs up. Caroline discussed her life as an English instructor at the University, having plenty of entertaining anecdotes to share. We listened attentively, chuckling at all her cute stories about misbehaving pupils. Meanwhile, I kept under-handing Ollie bits of burger.

Johanna caught me doing this and smiled slyly. *You really shouldn't do that,* her eyes said. *You'll turn that dog into a beggar.*

I shrugged. *As if he isn't already?*

The four of us chatted the day away --- the sun warm on our flesh. We were young. Happy. Divorce was the farthest thing from me and Johanna's minds. Our marriage wouldn't prove difficult for another decade yet. Caroline would live for another fifty years, Avery another sixty. But Ollie?

Ollie was going on fifteen years old in 1974. Despite the grey on his muzzle, he was spry and playful as a newborn pup.

Avery helped himself to a third bratwurst, as did I. Johanna picked a nickel-sized chunk off her hamburger and covertly held it beneath the table. Ollie trotted over, wagging his tail. He took the food from her fingers --- gently, ever so gently.

***

I raised my weary head from the table. My glass was empty. The clock on the wall read quarter to midnight. A clawing at the front door.

Groaning, I stumbled into the entryway and opened it.

It was raining heavily. Ollie, his scraggily coat completely soaked, trotted inside. His head hung low. Limping into the living room, he collapsed into his doggy bed. I grabbed a towel from the bathroom.

"You okay, boy?" I kneeled, inspecting his swollen paws. They were nearly soft-ball sized. He whined when I touched him and gazed up at me. All the malice I had observed in those eyes earlier was gone.

I gently toweled him, then brought him one of his chewies for a treat. "You don't really deserve it," I said, "after trying to take off my hand. But, here you go."

Ollie took the treat into his mouth, then stared up at me. Those eyes. So much said through those eyes. Hate, often. Happiness, rarely. At this very moment?

Regret. I could have sworn it.

Am I guilty of anthropomorphizing? Most folks would say so. But if you saw the wounded, utterly *human* expression in those eyes, you'd know what I mean.

"It's all right, boy. I forgive you."

Then I pointed a finger at him and said, "But if you ever bite me again, it's off to the damn pound. I don't care *what* Avery would think."

I went to bed and dreamed of happy days in the seventies. Johanna was feeding Ollie scraps beneath the table again. Only when I looked at what Ollie was lapping from her hand, I screamed.

Severed fingers. Bloody, with ragged bits of bone at the ends where they'd been torn from a hand. Ollie licked and lapped, gently taking the fingers into his mouth and shredding them. Johanna smiled at me, just as a throbbing pulse surged in my right hand. Slowly, I looked down.

All my fingers were gone, replaced with blood-spurting stumps.

I shot upright, drenched with sweat, awakened by my own screams. Dawn's first light shone through the bedroom window. Gazing down at my hand, I heaved a sigh.

Wriggled my fingers beneath the bandage.

***

The doorbell rung around ten a.m. I answered.

Curly blonde hair shrouded her slim face. Two blue eyes sparkled behind thick-frame glasses. "Hi Timothy," she smiled. "How've you been holding up?"

That tiny voice, spoken in her Boston accent, had always endeared me to her. Annette had been Avery's house keeper ever since Caroline began pushing up daisies.

"I'm doing okay," I replied. "Come in?"

"No, no, I don't want to be a bother. Just wanted to give you this."

She handed me a leather-bound photo album.

"*Oomph!*" I grunted, the book heavy as an iron anchor. "What's this?"

"Avery wanted you to have it," she smiled. "It was written in the will, but I wanted to keep it for a little while longer. Hope you don't mind. There's lots of good memories in there."

"No," I said, holding the album to my chest. "Of course I don't mind."

Annette's eyebrows knitted together. "What happened to your hand?"

"Oh, this? It's nothing. Was dicing up onions. Slipped the knife."

"Aww, poor thing . . ."

"It's no biggie, Annette. Honestly. And how are *you,* dear?"

"Well, I miss Av of course," she replied, crestfallen. "Otherwise, I'm doing all right. I visit him regularly. At the cemetery, I mean."

"He sure loved you, Annette."

"I know he did," she nodded. "He loved you too. And Ollie, of course. Speaking of Ollie, how has he adjusted?"

"Well enough," I shrugged. "Although, he's been a bit grumpy."

She nodded. "I guess *all* elders can be a bit grumpy. I know I certainly have *my* days."

"You sure you won't come in?" I asked.

"I have a doctor's appointment in half an hour. Otherwise, I would."

"Sure thing, Annette. Good luck at the Doc's. And thanks for the photos."

"Take good care, hon," she said, and leaned in to give me a peck on the cheek.

She descended the porch stairs, and I shut the door softly.

***

Flipping through the shrink-wrapped, pasteboard pages of that album made me laugh, *and* cry. The hours flew by with the album splayed over my lap. Ollie curled up in his bed and slept.

A photo of me and Avery playing beach volleyball --- Caroline had a whistle in her mouth, mid-blow, comically posing as a referee. A photo of Johanna and I, lounging in a hammock on a hot summer day. A photo of Ollie, staring directly into the lens. Avery and Caroline stood above, all big smiles, petting him.

They loved that dog. I guess I do too, most of the time. On the bottom-corner of the very last page, I discovered a newspaper clipping:

SPECIAL ONCE IN A LIFETIME OFFER!
SELECTBREED INC'S HIGH-TECH
WELL-BRED DOGS FOR SALE!!!
THEY'RE WELL-BEHAVED, INTELLIGENT,

& LIVE UP TO 4 TIMES LONGER THAN AVERAGE!
CALL 617-509-6962
(OFFER ALSO INCLUDES CATS, HAMSTERS, SNAKES & PARROTS).

The plastic wrap had prevented the faded yellow clipping from going completely to tatters.

SelectBreed Incorporated --- Add it to the list of infinite mysteries this universe has to offer: black holes, dark matter, quantum physics, the purpose of life (if any), God (if any), the fabric of space-time, the hard problem of consciousness, and, inevitably, SelectBreed Incorporated.

I'd done plenty of Google searches on SelectBreed in my time. I'd even done some personal detective work in downtown Boston, MA, where the 'company' had been located. Over the years, my inquiries had shed light on nothing, nada, zip.

I'd given up finding answers about Ollie's origins many years ago, believing my memories had led me astray. I clearly remembered the late Mr. Donahue mentioning the name *SelectBreed Inc.*, yet I'd second-guessed myself, figuring I'd heard wrong. And Avery, riddled with Alzheimer's for the last ten tears of his life, couldn't remember a damn about anything, so he was no use. As you grow older, one thing you come to understand --- memory is a fickle thing.

Could I have been searching around all that time for a name fabricated from my own imagination? That would explain, after all, why there seemed to be zero trace of SelectBreed's existence. Now, my memories were confirmed by an aged, yellowed advertisement, clipped out of a 1950's newspaper and saved for posterity.

I read it again, amazed:

SELECTBREED INC'S HIGH-TECH WELL-BRED DOGS FOR SALE!!!

I slammed the album shut with a sense of satisfaction. Ollie glanced up from the floor.

"So, you *do* exist after all."

Ollie groaned.

"What is it, boy? Hungry?"

He stared at me. No. Not hungry.

"Need to go outside? Potty?"

Ollie got up, slowly. His paws clicked toward the front door.

"Ah-ha," I said. I lay aside the album, and arose from the couch. Passing the dining room window, I noticed it'd gotten dark. Perusing the photos had passed the entire evening. I hadn't even had a drink in all that time.

Ollie clicked his way to the door. I would cut his nails if he didn't snap at me every time I tried. *Damn dog is going to run me ragged.* My hand reached for the door knob. Ollie growled.

I looked down. He bared his teeth.

"What's *wrong* with you?" I said. "I thought you wanted to go outside?"

Ollie whimpered, trotting back into the living room. I frowned. "You are becoming more bi-polar by the day," I told him. When I turned back to the door, it was open. Two men stood in the doorway, wearing ski masks. One of them pushed hard, knocking me flat on my back. They slammed the door behind them.

"Who the hell do you guys think---"

I suddenly found myself staring down the barrel of a gun, then gazing up into the invader's icy blue eyes. His ski mask was dark red. His partner's was black.

"Whatever you guys want," I said, "take it."

"We intend to," said Blue Eyes. "Now, is there anyone else in the house?"

I shook my head. There was Ollie, of course, but he was just an old, cowardly dog with arthritis. He hardly counted.

"You're positive?"

"Yes."

"Good."

The one wearing the black ski mask shouldered a large laundry bag. He went around the room, snatching antique items off shelves and dropping them in. My silver candelabra, handed down through family generations, sat as the centerpiece of my dining table. That went into the bag first thing.

The man disappeared into the kitchen. Cupboard doors slammed. Pots and pans rattled and clanked. His partner kept the gun on me.

I lay there on the floor. My back hurt. I looked up into the man's blue eyes. No wrinkles. Bags, yes, heavy purple ones. But no wrinkles.

"Stop fucking looking at me like that," he growled, shoving the gun against the bridge of my nose.

"You're making a mistake, young man," I said.

"So are you, if you keep running your mouth. Shut up!"

His partner entered the room, dragging a half-full bag.

"You being good, old man?" he asked.

I raised my middle-finger in reply. He laughed high-pitched, like a hyena. "Keep your aim on this guy," he said. "He's a feisty old bastard!"

I wasn't able to catch eyes with the bag-man, but his voice sounded older. A potbelly protruded from his black sweater. He went into the living room. Clattering and smashing noises followed. Things were being torn off the walls. Antique collectibles. Ornate picture frames. My Sony stereo would go too, I was quite sure.

"So, old fart," said Blue Eyes. "How long you been livin' here?"

I shook my head. First he'd told me to shut up. Now he wanted to bullshit.

Kids. They're stupid. None of them know what the hell they want. None of them know anything.

"What's the matter, old man?" he teased. "Scared to talk?"

I laughed. He thought he was scary. The hammer clicked back.

"Don't fucking laugh at me!" he shrieked.

Okay. This time he *was* scary. Suddenly the din from the living room ceased. A moment of silence, then I heard the man in there murmuring in a low voice.

The kid cocked his head, listening.

Then erupted the screams. Agonized, painful screams -- as if the thief in my living room were being torn apart.

Blue Eyes ran for the living room. I caught his heel and yanked. He fell, smashing his nose into the hardwood floor. His gun skittered across the room. He held his bleeding nose and sobbed.

His partner, the bag-man, ran through the doorway (this time, without the bag). Ollie was literally on his ass, sinking teeth into the flesh of his buttocks. The man howled, jerking left and right, attempting to escape Ollie's locked jaws. He collapsed flailing onto his side, bumping the dining table to topple onto the floor with a crash.

Ollie managed to turn the man over onto his back, paws on his chest, teeth gnashing. The man hammered at Ollie's nose with his fists. I watched, stunned by the grisly horror of it all. Ollie bit the man's face --- again and again. Blood gushed, all dark red and sticky.

Then the screams ceased as suddenly as if someone hit 'mute' on a remote.

Ollie's snout was buried inside the man's neck. Exposed jugular veins pulsed. The thief's eyes were wide, lifeless. Ollie backed away from the body; his snout, face and chest coated in red. He was gazing over at me now.

Those eyes, those sad, knowing eyes.

I looked toward my left. Blue Eyes had torn his mask off, one hand holding his busted nose, the other holding his gun again. He wasn't pointing it at me.

The kid pulled back the hammer.

I opened my mouth, about to shout for him to put it down.

He pulled the trigger. Ollie's chest exploded in a dark red burst. The dog --- my dog --- dropped to the ground next to the bag-man's mutilated body. The kid, his pale, gaunt face stricken with horror, scrabbled to his feet and escaped out the front door. I crawled over to Ollie. Approaching sirens drifted through the gun-smoke air. My ears rang.

Ollie's side rose and fell with shallow, irregular breaths. A high whine sounded from his throat. I wiped away my tears and inspected his wounds. The bullet had penetrated his chest, exiting about the middle of the rib cage. A pool of blood seeped beneath him, and within the blood were not only exposed organs, but circuit boards, frayed wires, and electric cells. I was too saddened to feel surprised. To me, it didn't matter what Ollie was composed of. He was my dog, and he had saved my life.

"Ollie," I whispered. "Why'd you do that? You should've just let those assholes take what they wanted . . . Oh, Ollie. I'm *sorry.*"

I laid my head against Ollie's face. Kissed him. When I raised my head, he was gone; the slim white spark in the back of his pupils now faded into black gloss.

***

I don't know how many days passed, lost in that drunken stupor --- a man without a friend, and now, without a dog. Dead Avery. Dead dog. My ex-wife, Johanna, might as well be dead too. She's nearly as old as I am. It'll be any day now, for either of us.

Getting out of bed in the morning is a difficult task. I have a suspicion a day will come when there'll be no morning at all. No sun. Just perpetual midnight.

I ache all over, and my back still hurts from the fall. Head, knees, and hands hurt these days too. Don't know why. Old, I guess. Just like Ollie was. Pretty soon I'll be limping with swollen feet every time it rains. I'll click about the house, whining like the old dog that I am.

The whiskey is in short supply.

***

Annette came by. She does every day now, it seems. She sits at my dining table, even though the floor is stained with blood. The police finally caught the young guy, Blue Eyes, and threw him in jail. Good, I suppose. Although, I don't really care either way. I just want my dog and my best friend back, and the two may or may not be the same thing.

Annette held my hand in hers. She never offers solutions to my ills, which I appreciate. She just asks questions, listens, and nods.

"You should shave, hon," she said, stroking my face.

"I think I will. Just for you, dear."

"That's a good boy," she winked.

"I'm seventy-five years old. Hardly a boy."

She laughed. "Well, there's still time to be a boy if you want. Age is just a number, Tim."

"It sure doesn't feel like a number. It feels like hell and sorrow."

A small smile dawned upon her lips.

"What?" I asked.

"Nothing. I just hope you find happiness, Tim Bently. You're a good man."

"Thanks," I replied. "Does that mean you might enjoy having dinner with me?"

She slapped my arm, laughing. *Oh, you old scamp.*

She left shortly after, but I noticed she hadn't exactly said, 'No'.

***

A rapping at my door. I got out of bed, hungover, and shuffled downstairs. The clock on the wall read six a.m. Hints of pre-dawn light shone through the windows. The knocking continued.

I paused before opening the door. The two robbers barging through and knocking me over flashed through my mind. Then I remembered, robbers don't knock. Jehovah's Witnesses do, though. I groaned, unsure which group I detested more, thieves or evangelists.

I opened the door. No one stood there with a bible, asking if I'd been saved. Instead, it was a tall, broad shouldered man with short blonde hair, wearing a charcoal grey suit. In his hands, a box.

"Good morning, Sir," he said.

"I'm not interested in what you're selling," I replied, wiping sleep from my eyes.

"Not selling anything, Mr. Bently," he smiled. "This is a gift."

"Listen," I said. "This community has been awfully kind enough with all the condolence baskets I've received over the past week. I appreciate it, but I'm afraid I can't accept anymore."

The door was nearly closed before he pushed it back open.

"You don't understand," he interjected, releasing a small, breathy laugh. "This is a *replacement.*"

I studied the man's face. It was a kind, somewhat strange face. His eyes were smart, and his complexion told me he spent a lot of time in-doors. "We apologize for the deterioration of the last one," he said. "But that model was created in the 1950's! We've come a long way in gen-tech since then, Mr. Bentley. We believe our latest model should last at least *two* full human generations --- with very minor physical deteriorations! Of course, only time will show."

He shoved the box into my arms.

"Hey! But I don't---"

"Forgive me," he interrupted. "But I can't help noticing how *old* you are, Mr. Bentley. Be sure to have your will in order." He nodded at the box in my hands. "It'll require a safe home oncc you're gone."

He turned, walking briskly to the nondescript white van parked on the street. Exhaust fumes spilled into the chilly air as he drove away. I shook my head and went inside. Talk about people who don't take 'no' for an answer.

I set the box on the table, pulled away the tape, and opened the flaps. I reached in and lifted him out: a sleeping, chocolate colored puppy with white and brown spots all about its hindquarters, much like Ollie.

No, I reconsidered. *Exactly like Ollie.*

Written on the box's inside flap:

SelectBreed Incorporated Wishes You the Best with Your New, Life-Long Companion!

The dog opened its sleepy eyes, then made a cute squeaking sound that I suppose was a bark. I held him to my chest, mildly surprised to find my eyes brimming. When the tears inevitably spilled, the puppy lapped them up, and I laughed.

"What a fine doggy," I told him. "I'll name you Ollie Jr. Not very original, perhaps, but fitting. Don't you think?"

I set Ollie Jr. on the floor, where he immediately unleashed a stream of urine. Apparently SelectBreed hadn't thought to genetically alter potty habits, but that was okay. Ollie Jr. and I would work on that.

***

He was potty-trained within one week. I'm rather proud of that.

I've poured all the remaining alcohol in my house down the drain, making a resolution never to pick up the bottle again. I'm hoping Ollie Jr. will hold me accountable. He's proud of me for getting on the wagon --- or so I like to think, and I'd hate to disappoint.

Tonight is a special night. Annette is sitting across from me at the table, her face bronze in the candlelight. Blonde curls frame her lovely face, and her azure eyes are deep and full as a luscious spring.

Ollie Jr. chews on a toy beneath the table. Life is good for all of us, it seems.

And as a seventy-five year old man, I've never felt so young.

EVERYTHING IS BROKEN

Highway 120 is a long stretch of asphalt slicing through the hot Arizona desert. I began to nod, a consequence of being on the road for the last nine hours. The cozy heat of the sun and lullaby hum of tires on pavement didn't help matters.

Suddenly, I jolted awake. There'd been a dramatic switch from black asphalt to bumpy gravel road. I widened my eyes, slapped my face, and rolled down the window.

Checking the rearview, I could no longer see that black ribbon of highway. Nothing around but cacti, tumbleweeds and bronze desert.

Jesus! How long was I asleep?

With the highway nowhere in sight, it must've been at least a couple minutes. Somehow, I'd drifted onto a branching road instead of straight into the ditch. I was just glad not to have rammed into somebody, or worse.

Ahead of me, a green sign gleamed in the sun --- mounted on a rusty, crooked stand. Part of me wanted to turn the Buick around and re-locate the highway, but I was tired. I needed somewhere to rest. A hotel, preferably. Two whole states remained between myself and a summer vacation with family I hadn't visited in ages. The timeliness of my arrival, it seemed, would now have to settle for *fashionably late.*

Slowing my speed, I peered through the windshield at the crooked sign:

WELCOME TO BROKEN SPRING

POP. 321

"Broken Spring." I read aloud, chuckling. "Sounds promising."

I jostled in my seat, running over the road's myriad potholes. In the distance, an immense cloud of dust particles hovered near to the ground. I could scarcely discern the outlines of houses and buildings.

Despite the cab rocking over the roughness of the road, my eyes threatened to close again. I turned on the radio to keep awake. Scanned the stations.

A hissing of static filled the cab. Not a voice, nor note of music came through.

Bummer.

I switched off the dial.

Then:

RUG-RUG-RUG-RUG-RUG-RUG!

The orthodox tic of the Buick's engine became a low, rugged chug. I frowned, checking my gauges.

The check engine light blinked.

Well, shit.

The steering wheel vibrated roughly in my hands.

God damn it, now what?

KA-POP-KA-POP-KA-POP! Miniature black clouds in my rearview merged with the trail of gravel dust floating in the hot air.

The engine sputtered and died.

"Son of a . . . " I turned the ignition key several times. The engine refused to catch. After several attempts, the damned thing flooded. When I picked up my phone to call roadside service, the screen was black.

"*Fuck!*" I chucked the phone onto the passenger seat, cursing myself for neglecting to keep it charged.

Climbing out of the car, I was reminded how much I hate Arizona. The sun was hotter than a whore's knob on payday and the air was miserably dry. I debated whether or not to pop the hood. I'd never been mechanically inclined. Gazing over my shoulder, black smoke began to plume out from beneath the Buick's hood. Whatever had gone awry, I was almost positive I didn't know how to fix it.

I grabbed my rolling suitcase from the backseat, then headed toward town.

Sure hope Broken Spring has a mechanic.

The sun was hot on my face and shoulders. I swallowed a lump in my parched throat, hoping to purchase a refreshing beverage at the town gas station.

If they *had* a gas station.

The tiny plastic wheels of my suitcase rattled over gravel. As I drew close, I found I could no longer observe the cloud of desert haze around the town. For I had entered the cloud and was now part of it. The air swirled with grit, spackling my face and arms and making it impossible to open my mouth without eating a sand-sandwich.

I ambled down Main Street, sweat dripping down my forehead. My tongue stuck to the roof of my mouth, sounding like Velcro every time I peeled it away. Houses lined both sides of the street.

Well, not exactly *houses*. More like shacks with rusted aluminum walls and partially dilapidated roofs. Children's faces peered out through cupola windows, their cheeks grubby. Sand speckled their clothes and hair. Their faces were horribly ugly, warped, misshapen. The result of inbreeding, I thought, and despite the desert heat, a cold shiver coursed through me.

Splitting off from Main on the right was Desecration Street. Along this grimy stretch of buckling asphalt stood an old brick bank building with shattered windows. Next to it, a post office the size of a broom closet. Adjacent to that, a police station with a rusted Queen Vic propped on cinderblocks out front, no tires on its rims. Further down, a dingy pub. Its sign --- *Broken*

Wing Saloon --- hung cockeyed on a chain, featuring a one-winged crow as its emblem.

Vanquished Avenue branched left from Main.

Interesting place. Desecration Street. Vanquished Avenue. What's next, Shatter Road? How about Splinter Lane?

My jaw clenched, baring the heat, grit, and frustration.

On Vanquished Ave was (*thank God!*) a gas station called *Vic's Stop 'n Stay.*

Ludwig's Tire Shop stood at its opposite --- a place where men in grease-coated overalls cursed, spat brown, chunky tobacco and bitched about their wives. They wiped their hands on grease rags religiously, yet never made them clean.

I crossed onto Vanquished, heading toward *Vic's Stop 'n Stay*. Two cobwebbed gas pumps stood cockeyed from the parking lot's cracked foundation. I paused, squinting up at the station sign. *Stop 'n Stay. Isn't it supposed to be Stop 'n Go?*

"Weird fuckin' place," I muttered, entering the station.

Clunk! The cowbell on the door dully announced my entrance. It was sweltering inside the pathetically small station --- even hotter in here than out in the sun, odd as that was. Peering above aisles of multi-colored snacks, I searched for the refrigerator banks.

"Welcome, stranger." A man with thick stubble on his chin, only one arm, and impeccably clean glasses greeted me.

"Hello Vic," I said, noting his name tag.

"If you're lookin' for a bathroom, I'm afraid it's out-of-order. Plumbing is fucked."

"Just need some water," I replied. "Maybe a Gatorade."

"Over there." He nodded toward a single refrigerator in the back corner.

I walked over, stood before the glass door with Lime Gatorade behind it --- the only flavor available. Not my favorite, but beggars can't be choosers. I opened the door, expecting that cold whoosh of air to bring goosebumps to my sweaty skin. But the refrigerator was the same miserable temp as everything else --- hot, hot, hot.

I grabbed a warm bottle of Gatorade. Returned to the front desk.

"Excuse me?"

Vic gazed up from a very literary magazine called *Big Jugs*.

"Your fridge isn't working," I said.

He stared at me blankly. "Uh-huh?"

I shrugged. Opened my wallet. Laid down three bucks. He took the cash with his one hand, slid it into a petty bag, and dug through the coins.

"Why don't you use that cash register?" I nodded toward the old register on the counter.

"Don't work." Vic handed me the change.

"Sounds like this place could use some maintenance."

The one-armed clerk tossed back his head and laughed. His nostrils flared and it occurred to me his perfectly clean glasses weren't clean at all.

Empty frames.

I frowned. "Something I say strike you funny?"

"Ahh, shit!" He waved his hand dismissively. "Don't act like a horse's ass, friend. Ya ain't from around here, is all."

"Clearly."

"Well, y'see," he said, stifling his smile, "there ain't a maintenance man 'round these parts. Wouldn't do no good if we had one, anyway. See, Broken Spring abides by a whole *different* set of laws."

"What kind of laws?"

"Physics, boy! What them scientists call, En-tro-pee."

Before I could ask what the hell he was talking about, the entrance bell made a sad *clunk*, and a tall, hulking man in uniform entered. A scuffed star was pinned to his shirt-pocket: *Sheriff Brokaw. 55103859.*

There's too many digits on his badge, I mused. *. . . weird.*

The northernmost tip of the star was chipped, too.

"Howdy stranger!" Brokaw's voice was gritty as desert sand.

"Hello."

"What brings ya to these parts, stranger?"

I grabbed my purchase from the counter, unscrewed the cap. "Gatorade," I replied, then took three enormous gulps. Despite its warmness, it soothed my throat.

The handcuffs on Brokaw's utility belt rattled as he laughed. "Well, sorry it's not s'cold. One day maybe ol' Vic here will get that fridge up and runnin'."

Vic scoffed and set a tin of Grizzly Wintergreen on the scratched glass counter. Brokaw brushed past me, laid down cash. Before Vic could even count back change, Brokaw had tucked a pinch of tobacco into the bottom right of his cheek.

The sheriff stared at me while keeping his palm open for Vic. He grinned with teeth all crooked and brown-yellow. His breath wafted over. Smelled like dog shit.

"Welcome to Broken Spring, boy," he grinned. "Enjoy your stay."

Then a stream of diarrhea brown tobacco launched from his mouth, landing on the scuffed linoleum mere inches from my shoes. I gazed down at the translucent brown liquid, then up at Brokaw. His amiable grin was tinged with scorn.

"You sure have a funny way of welcoming people, Sherriff," I replied, dryly.

Then I backed out the door, and the bell *clunked* as it closed.

***

Christ, what a town . . . I better watch myself. Make sure none of the locals (locos?) try anything with me.

The grease-stained men across the street wore peculiar smiles as I approached the open garage door. Lining both sides of the door were ancient rusted-out cars --- paint-peeled and sun-bleached as the bones of a beached fish. Flat tire stacks. Orange-tinged shrapnel sticking up out of the sand like abstract metal sculptures.

Above the garage, a sign with faded red lettering:

The Junk Punks

Classy. I bared my best P.R. smile as I stood before the door. Half a dozen men gazed up from under the hoods and chassis of damaged vehicles. One of them, lying on a rolling-bench, glanced up, shook his head, then returned to torqueing bolts beneath a severely dented, wood paneled station wagon.

A 'junk punk' with round, cracked spectacles and a tuft of gray hair offered his hand.

"How-ee, pawwer!" he said. "My ame iz Ahm."

Despite the man's speech impediment, I was fairly sure of what he'd said.

"Salutations, Tom." I shook his hand. My palm came away thick with black grease. I frowned, wiping my hand on my jeans.

"Uhm." I said, "My car broke down about quarter a mile out of town. Don't know what's wrong with it, but it won't start."

Tom nodded impatiently, gesturing for me to *go on, go on.*

"Anyway," I continued. "Think you and your guys could fix it? I'm on a cross-country trip, and would like to get back on the road soon."

Tom opened his mouth in a child-like smile, revealing toothless purple gums. In back of his throat was a blackened lump where his tongue used to be.

"Aw yeh," said Tom, drooling from one corner of his mouth. "We fik eet, awright."

I nodded. "Excellent. You own a tow truck, I'm guessing? Cause there's no way anyone could drive it here. It's dead as . . . well, dead."

"Ahh me your eeez."

I handed him my keys.

"Ome ack een a houwr!"

"Thanks a bunch," I said, and made myself scarce.

***

Bellied up to the bar at Broken Wing Saloon, blood drew from my lip after cutting it on a chipped shot glass. The fat, sweaty bartender with an impressive row of jowls and an eyepatch laughed when I confronted him.

"This'll fix ya up," he said and poured me another shot, this time to the brim. "Avoid the chipped spot this time." I shook my head, yet nonetheless accepted the free shot.

Now, standing on the corner of Desolation Street and Main, I felt good. Not drunk, but relaxed. Not even the heat bothered me anymore. It wouldn't be long before it was dark anyway, and the desert gets cold at night.

Squinting my eyes, I spied something creeping up Main Street. Distant figures surrounded a large, metal object. *A mirage?* I peered into the faraway haze.

No. Not a mirage.

The junk punks were towing my vehicle into town. Not with a tow-truck, but with their bodies. In the fashion of two horses drawing a carriage, two men with chains attached to the front bumper pulled with all their might. Three men pushed in back, while another leaned inside the open window and steered the wheel. Cursing and grunting, they rolled the vehicle up the street, then finally into their garage.

My car was in worse shape than I'd left it. The windshield sported an enormous crack and the hood was dented. I gritted my teeth, knowing I'd make *damned* sure those grease monkeys wouldn't get away with damaging my vehicle. They'd reimburse me. Preferably with a wad of cash.

Fists clenched, I stalked over to the Junk Punks. Just as I was about to confront them, one of the men pulled a rope, and the garage door slammed down on its squealing rollers.

I pounded on the door, which rattled violently against its steel track. "Open up, damn it!"

A side door on the garage staccato-creaked as it opened. The junk punks, still wiping their hands with grease rags, filed out like a redneck version of the seven dwarves.

Tom was the last one out. The others each went their way, scattering in various directions. I marched over to Tom, who stood gazing at the setting sun.

"Hey! Want to tell me what you guys did to my windshield? How about that dent in my hood?"

Tom looked at me. Blinked.

I heaved a sigh. "Look, where are you guys going? I thought you said you'd have my car fixed in an hour?"

Tom shook his head. "Ime oo go ome! We fiik ii ooo-morrow."

The man sauntered away, gray hair waving in a breezeless air. The red-gold sun dipped into the bronze landscape. I stood alone on Vanquished Avenue. Across the cracked and weedy road, Vic placed a *CLOSED* sign in the station window.

Heading north on Main Street, I passed dozens of ramshackle tin-can houses before coming upon a fractured parking lot. There, resting upon the asphalt, a series of trashy aluminum trailer homes hitched together. A small building off to the left sported a big sign:

HEARTBREAK HOTE *L*

VACANCY.

The 'L' hung at an odd, crooked angle upon the sign.

Not exactly promising. But where else was there to sleep, except some vacant alleyway? I walked over to the small brick building, stood before the cracked receptionist window, and reserved a trailer for an overnight. The clerk behind the glass frowned and cocked his head every time I spoke. He had one ear. A lump of burn tissue folded over the canal was all that remained of the other.

I accepted the room key, mumbling false gratitude.

Upon entering the trailer, my jaw dropped. I knew the room would be lousy --- I just didn't know it'd be *this* lousy.

A bundle of sheets and blankets lay unkempt upon the mattress, as if there'd been a wrestling match. Then I noticed the large, dried come stain upon a turquoise pillow. The people who'd last occupied the bed clearly had done more than wrestle.

I snagged a corner of the pillow and tossed it on the floor, the stain facing down. The bedside table was grubby with fingerprints, used needles, and two crusty spoons. A crack ran through the lamp's dusty shade. A small trash bin beside the table had gone unemptied. Inside were bloody tissue, cigarette butts and empty beer bottles.

Across the small space of the room, a fat 1980's Toshiba television squatted upon a dresser. Only jagged shards remained in the frame. Inside the gutted out box were bizarre cardboard cutouts depicting the crucifixion of Jesus Christ.

Except Christ hadn't any legs, and the cross to which he'd been nailed was cockeyed. At least a dozen cardboard people stood gathered around Him --- all featuring physical deformities: missing ears, noses, eyes, and limbs.

Easily the most blasphemous display I'd ever seen. Shoving the television around so the grotesque display faced the wall, I then looked for a bathroom. It was on my right, next to a closet.

I didn't want to go in there for fear of what may've been left behind in the tub . . . or the toilet. Still, I had to pee. I took a deep breath and entered, prepared for the worst.

The tiny restroom was surprisingly clean. Although when I tried the sink faucet, nothing came out. The toilet had a limp flush-lever. The tub was also non-functional. A dark red stain tattooed its basin.

Returning to the bed, I inspected the blanket and sheets for anything gross. The bundle of linen was stained dark with blood. There was also a brown, crusty substance. Probably feces. My nose scrunched up, and my stomach roiled with disgust. I tossed the linen onto the floor beside the come-stained pillow. The mattress, thankfully, appeared unsoiled. The box spring squealed as I lay down, using my hands for a pillow. Soon, moonlight shone between the window's dusty Venetian blinds and I drifted asleep.

Dreams of hobo angels with broken halos. Limb-deficient devils with snapped horns. Screaming infants swaddled in grease rags, their pudgy faces twisting like that infamous subject in Edvard Munch's The Scream.

Moaning, snarling noises echoed out of the rusted shacks of Broken Spring. The residents ravaged each other in the night, clutching, grasping, their hands devoid of fingers. Sagging flesh quivering with pleasure. Naked stubs twitching like dead, fat, galvanized maggots. The King's signature song cycled on perpetual repeat --- the notes crippled, shambling down the streets and drowning in back alleys before rising again, and falling, and rising like a garbage-strewn wave upon a sea of entropy.

I'm so lonely, baby, *the King crooned off-key.* I'm so lonely, I could die.

Torn-up, desperate howls.

Broken tongues in a wordless dance of desolation.

The all-consuming negation of life by Decadence.

The entire universe . . . winding down, down, down.

I snapped awake on the bare mattress, covered with sweat and gooseflesh. I caressed my face and body, making sure I was still intact, that I still had all my limbs.

Making sure I was unbroken.

It was night in the desert, and the desert was cold.

***

Checking out of Heartbreak Hotel at 9 a.m., the one-eared receptionist insisted I stay another night. I told him I'd rather have a marlin spike driven through my forehead, *thank you very much.* Ambling down the street on my way to the Junk Punks', hoping like hell they were working on the

Buick, I noticed Sheriff Brokaw. He stood outside Broken Wing Saloon. Chipped glass of bourbon in his hand.

Brokaw grinned, raising his glass. A trickle of blood ran from his upper lip. Despite the day's already ravenous heat, I shivered at his salutation.

The garage doors were open. The punks worked diligently on a vehicle --- just not mine. Tom stood by the doorway, bullshitting with the men in his broken tongue.

"Hey," I said. "How's my car coming?"

Tom turned, regarded me with raised eyebrows. "Aw yeh! Aw unn!"

"*All done?*" I asked, flabbergasted. "It's running?"

The man grinned, the purple half-tongue wiggling in his mouth like the tail of an excited dog. I averted my eyes.

"Iss way," Tom said, and I followed him around the corner, taking a left onto Crippled Street.

"Why'd you park it way down here?" I asked.

"Ooo ee."

You'll see. I took a deep breath, attempting patience. We were passing through the residential area of Broken Spring. Shacks of rusted metal grating, aluminum siding, and rebar lined the street. Cracked doll heads atop fence posts stuck out of the sand, like some deranged tribute to the Dark Ages.

Families peered through the windows --- those open spaces within rusting walls. Some were eating breakfast out of cupped, grimy hands. Others read (or pretended to read) sections of torn newspaper. My heart trembled at the sound of an infant crying.

That a child should be born in a place like this, a desert ghetto populated by unenlightened half-wits, was depressing. The crying reminded me of last night's dreams. The hairs on my arms stood on end.

We rounded a bend, turning onto Wreckage Road. Tom halted on the shattered sidewalk. Pointed at a shack.

"Here oo awwr!"

The familiar white doors of my Buick stood vertical and half-buried in the sand, forming a small entrance. The walls consisted of my hood, trunk, and floor paneling. A slab of brittle plywood formed the ceiling. Situated within the walls, my tires served for windows. The rims lay in the sand before the shack, like hillbilly lawn ornaments.

My mouth hung open. Promptly shutting it, I turned to Tom. He stood there, arms crossed, grinning those horrid purple gums --- obviously proud of what he'd done. My fists clenched.

Getting nose to nose with him, I glared into those dumb, blank eyes.

"You're going to reimburse me," I told him. "You're going to give me $10,000, which is what my car was worth. And if you refuse, I'll beat the *shit* out of you."

Tom tilted back his head, Adam's apple bobbing as he laughed. My blood boiled. I threw a right fist and clocked him square in the mouth.

Tom slumped to his knees, then looked up, rubbing his jaw.

"Wha you ooo at for?"

"Because you're *fucking* with me," I shouted. "Trying to scare me and make it seem like I can't leave this God forsaken place. Well, it's not going to work, you stupid redneck!"

"Buh I uil you a ouz!"

"You *what?!*"

"I uil you a ouz!"

"That's not a house, you dummy. That's my *car* arranged into a *hobo shack!* Now, if you try anything more with me, I'm not only going to beat the crap out of you, I'll *kill you.* Got that?"

He nodded like a wounded puppy, his lower lip sticking out.

"Good," I said. "Now, I'm off to see the sheriff."

I left the man kneeling there in the sand, sobbing like a baby. His pitiful cries carried from three blocks away, as I approached Broken Spring's Police Station.

The front door was locked. Peering into the cracked side windows, it was dark as a tomb. I ventured down Desolation Street. If Sherriff Brokaw was anywhere to be found, it was probably at the Broken Wing Saloon, still slugging moonshine from his damaged glass.

Loyal flies hung around the entrance, chain-smoking cigarettes. Splintered buts and shattered bottles littered the sidewalk beneath their feet, a sort of party confetti for miscreants and low-lifes. A few were drinking in the street --- illegal in this state, but seeing as Brokaw himself was drinking out front earlier, I imagined this particular law wasn't enforced.

Someone shouted behind me:

"Well, well! Looky what we have here."

I spun around. Brokaw smiled crooked yellow teeth.

"Not only are ya a tourist," he said. "But a criminal as well, eh?"

"Criminal?" I frowned. "The hell are you on about, Sheriff? I haven't broken any laws. Those people up there are drinking in the street. Not to mention one of your resident mechanics outright demolished my car. That's destruction of private property, just so you know, Sheriff."

A growl escaped from behind Brokaw's grated teeth. His fists clenched and unclenched. I hadn't noticed the missing thumb and pinky finger on each hand until now.

"All right, city boy," Brokaw scowled, drawing his gun. "You're comin' down to the station."

"Bullshit!" I spat. "I haven't *done* anything. You have no right to arrest me."

"I'm the *sheriff.*" A terrible, ominous grin spread across Brokaw's face. "I do what I want in this here town. And what I want . . . is *you.*"

I glanced in all directions, searching for a possible escape route. There were none. Only derelict buildings. Crumbling foundations. Shattered windows.

Reluctantly, I held up my hands.

"*Pussy.*" Brokaw guffawed, then spit out a long, muddy stream of chew. He returned the gun to his holster. Handcuffs jangled as he unhooked them from his belt.

This is your moment, I thought, then broke into a run.

"Hey!" Brokaw crowed. "Get the *fuck* back here!"

I sprinted down the street, barreling through the crowd of drunkards outside Broken Wing Saloon. None attempted to grab me. They were either too drunk or apathetic.

BLAM!

The shot rang through the air as one of the drunkard's heads exploded. Warm blood and brains littered the pavement and the left side of my face. My heart hammered in my chest as I continued running, turning a corner, then---

BLAM! Specks of rouge powder flew off the building beside me. I sneezed, having accidentally inhaled some of it. Sprinting down the street, I rounded another corner, darted down a foul-smelling alleyway, then kept on until my lungs threatened to burst.

Finally, I'd left Broken Spring in the dust. I gazed over my shoulder at the town's jagged silhouette. Faint shouts echoed in the distance.

I needed to keep moving. Brokaw would be on me in no time, most likely with a posse. The residents would hunt me down with sharp pieces of rebar, shrapnel and who knew what else.

The sun was mercilessly hot. My throat was parched. My head ached. My clothes were soaked with sweat. The sight of endless sand, cacti, and unclouded sky were token reminders that I just might die today.

Still, if I turned back, the troglodytes of Broken Spring would lynch me.

The town appeared like a shimmering mirage, especially with that buzzing cloud of particles surrounding it. I wasn't sure what sort of weather phenomena could create such a uniform cloud to hover perpetually around a random patch of desert. In truth, I doubted if weather could really do such a thing. To me, it implicated something . . . unnatural.

Something particularly grotesque, evil, and not of this world.

Turning toward the desert's vast expanse, I journeyed onward, wondering how many miles away civilization might be.

Suddenly, I halted in my tracks --- a sheering, twisting, agonizing pain radiated through my legs. Hot white sparks flooded my vision. I began to scream.

A loud crackling erupted beneath the flesh of my legs. The femurs, tibias, and bones in my feet shattered like glass.

My legs folded like a card table, every bone having been pulverized. My mouth collected hot, dry sand as I collapsed face-first onto the ground. Harrowing pain became all at once the ravager and ruler of my world. Using my arms, I crawled back toward Broken Spring.

A brutal force field, some invisible barrier between Broken Spring and the rest of the desert would not allow me to pass. At least, not without breaking every bone in my body. My heart palpitated as I sucked in the air, legs throbbing in agony.

Please, God, I prayed. *Help me. Help. Help!*

The outline of Broken Spring, the town I'd desperately longed to escape only moments ago, was farther away than ever. My legs burned as if on fire. I shrieked, tears rolling down my cheeks to evaporate in the hot sand. At last, I ceased crawling and lay my head down on my forearms. Exhaustion set in. The world blurred like a vision through fogged spectacles.

Then darkness cloaked my eyes.

***

"Shhhh, look! He's moving."

"Awake at last. What a sleepy head!"

"Shhhhhh!"

Voices drifted in and out. My eyes fluttered open, the doubled world soon merging into one. Men, women, and children took up nearly two dozen rickety church pews. Faces with missing ears, teeth, noses, eyes, limbs --- and most of all, minds --- stared up at me with reverence.

My hands burned and there was an uncomfortable tightness in my abdomen, but at least I didn't feel the agony in my legs anymore. From a great height, I peered about the room.

Golden light slanted through fractured stained-glass windows. The residents smiled with deranged joy. Rising from a slanted pew, Sheriff Brokaw ambled over to the altar stage. He smiled upward, hands on his hips.

"Took us awhile to perform the surgery," he beamed. "We thought ya wouldn't make it, but Doc here fixed ya right up. Ain't that right, Doc?"

On the farthest end of the front pew, a wrinkled woman with silver whiskers on her chin nodded satisfactorily. A black bag lay upon her lap. She opened it, holding it up for me to see.

Inside, the silver gleam of surgical instruments covered in blood.

A dread chill snaked up my spine.

Slowly, I gazed downward, afraid of what I would see. Thick strands of rope secured me to a wooden beam. My eyes trailed down the length of my body.

They did not trail far.

My legs were gone --- amputated mid-thigh. Two bandaged stubs remained, soaked dark with blood. My heart pounded. Blood throbbed in my temples with a rhythmic *whoosh-woosh, woosh-woosh*. I tried to scream, emitting only dry, screeching rasps.

Out of my peripheral, I glimpsed my hands. A long iron spike had been driven into both palms, fastening them to the wood. Blood trickled out of my hands, dripping upon the sermonizing platform below. The fucking bastards had *crucified* me. Rage and terror coursed through my veins.

"You miserable *cocksuckers!*" I shrieked.

A gasp from the crowd. I glared about the room, noting the familiar faces. Tom, the tongue-less mechanic. Vic, the one-armed clerk from the gas station. The family I'd glimpsed through their shack window yesterday evening. There was a husband and wife with dusty faces, torn clothes, and burn tissue covering their arms. The wife cradled a baby, presumably the one I'd heard crying earlier.

The baby's head was terribly misshapen and discolored. A deflated basketball with eyes, nose, and mouth. It began to cry.

This time, I did not feel sad for it, but disgust and rage. Its parents cooed at it, scratching its bulbous, jaundiced belly with grimy cuticles.

Brokaw laughed. "Well, city boy, now you can finally be of use to this town! Without them legs, you fit right in. Now, truth be told, we citizens of Broken Spring been needin' us some old-time religion. And you, my good friend, are goin' to *inspire us*."

The congregation rose up a cheer.

"You'll be up there on that crooked cross till the end of days," Brokaw continued, "and every Sunday we'll be gawkin' up at ya with awe and reverence. You've died for our sins, you see. The sin of thinkin' ourselves as being whole, unbroken, untarnished. The sin of tryin' to be better, more perfect than God Almighty. And no *one* or *thing* in this Creation is better or more perfect than God Almighty. Ain't that right?"

An eruption of hallelujahs boomed throughout the cramped church.

"Ya see, city boy? Your sacrifice to the power of Holy Entropy has paved our way to Salvation."

"You're fucking nuts!" I rasped. "You're *all* out of your god damned minds! Now, just . . . *please.* For God's sake, take me down. Just lay me out by the highway. I won't tell anyone a thing about this place. *I promise.*"

"Ain't no way." Brokaw shook his head. "Once you've entered Broken Spring, you never leave. Nobody ever has, in fact. And anyone that's tried . . . well. You know perfectly well what happened to them, don't ya?"

"Please," I shuddered with sobs. "Just get me down off this fucking cross. It's not right. None of this is right!"

"What's right is *Broken,*" Brokaw smiled. "And far as I can tell, you're about as broken as they come. Why, you should be *grateful,* city boy. Ain't everyday a person's welcomed with open arms into Broken Spring. It's a rare honor indeed."

My tears ceased and my pain faded, drowned out by a seething rage.

"*Fuck you, Brokaw,*" I growled, and spat blood.

Brokaw side-stepped. My bloody saliva splatted onto the stage. He clasped his hands in prayer, grinning more maniacally than ever.

Turning to the congregation, he spoke with the tenor and cadence of a southern Baptist.

"Everyone please stand and join me in sacred prayer."

The residents stood, all except those without legs. The deformed infant suckled contentedly at his mother's filthy breast. The father watched his child suckle and massaged his crotch, aroused at the sight. Tom smiled, waving at me from the back row as if he were an old pal. Vic adjusted his lens-less glasses, bowing his head in solemnity.

"We humbly thank you, God Almighty," Brokaw spoke, "For delivering unto us this miracle of decadence. For Everything is Brokenness, and Brokenness is Everything. To your great universal law of Entropy, we give utmost thanks. Amen."

"Amen!" the congregation returned.

An eruption of vile curses spilled from my lips, attempting to disrupt this grotesque mockery of Christianity.

I went ignored. Brokaw's tenor and passion slowly built into a shrill, ranting ode to His Holiness in Entropy. The faces of the congregation illumined with the light of madness, their eyes wide, empty, and hypnotized.

After a long time, I ceased screaming and writhing, accepting my place upon this crooked cross with grim resignation. My mind began to wander --- a means of escaping this endless pain and humiliation. And I remembered yesterday evening . . . what seems like such a long, long time ago. Driving down Highway 120, attempting not to fall asleep. Now, closing my teary eyes, I pray that when I open them, I will find myself somewhere else.

Somewhere far away from the cursed, impossible town of Broken Spring.

Somewhere untouched by the decay of entropy.

Somewhere I could safely lay my head, and call home.

The Stories behind the Stories

Some folks (the peculiar kind, such as yours truly) enjoy learning the process and circumstances behind how stories are written. If you're not that particular sort of reader, then by all means, close up the book. You've accompanied me this far, and I appreciate you greatly.

Go home. Drive safe. Consider sleeping with the lights on tonight.

As for the rest of you, the show isn't quite over. Allow me to draw back the curtain. This is the story behind the stories . . .

First, the setting:

An old, shut-down cheese factory in an undisclosed location of the Midwest. The place is chock full of equipment, yet empty of people. A sour, musty odor hangs in the air. Pipes rattle and clank. Rainwater trickles from the leaky ceiling. Occasionally, someone moans with sorrowful agony, yet there’s no readily available explanation for its origin.

Then, there's me.

The writer.

The security guard.

I work the graveyard shift, patrolling the crumbling hallways and the leaky warehouse and the damp evaporator rooms. Checking gauges on the gigantic, rusty boiler, hoping it doesn't blow up in my face. Eyeing the security monitors, assuring there aren't any break-ins or acts of vandalism. Not that there's much to worry about in these regards. The factory is located in a quiet town of no more than 800 people. Nobody comes around. Outside these walls, a perpetually wintery silence settles over the land, and the sun dips beneath the hills.

When I'm not patrolling, I'm writing. Nearly every one of the stories in this book (save for *The Typewriter*) were written in this eroding ruin of a once-thriving business. I wrote them from sunset until deep into the early hours.

This was before a new company swooped in and purchased the place --- Lord knows why, with all the expensive renovations they'll have to make --- canceling security services immediately.

With just a snap of the fingers, I was out of a job. In the course of a year and two months of my working there, I produced two books worth of stories. You're reading one of them now.

Well. On to the meat of this thing, shall we?

The prime cuts.

The Day the Stories Died

I believe stories are what make us human. Take them away, and humanity loses its essence.

It is imagination and art which makes life worth living. Everything else is struggle, strife, survival --- necessity, in a word. But as Oscar Wilde wrote, "All art is quite useless."

Art is useless because it is unnecessary, and delightfully so. It is precisely this unnecessary aspect of art which makes it beautiful and luxurious.

Where would we be without our favorite books and stories? I wanted to illustrate viscerally the importance and, yes, even go so far as to communicate a 'necessity', for stories in our lives.

Art may not be vital to life, but it is vital to a life *worth living*. It's an important point, I feel, which is why I've placed this story first in the collection.

Independence Day in Holebrim, Texas.

I owe Joe Lansdale a debt of gratitude. The first book of Lansdale's I'd ever read, a story collection entitled, *High Cotton: Stories*, made quite an impression on me. His voice and style became permanently lodged in my brain. As a result, my interpretation of Lansdale's narrative style just erupted one night, and I merged with my main character completely. It took only two days to complete the first draft, knowing I had a hot one.

Originally published in a very fine anthology book entitled, *Scare Me,* from Esskaye Books, a UK-based publisher.

The Drip

Every once in a while, a writer pens a story which absolutely takes him by surprise. *The Drip* is one of those stories. A dark, unnerving tone underscores the entire narrative. I don't know where that tone came from, but it's different from my other stories.

The Drip features a recurring theme in my work --- alcoholism. I'm not an alcoholic, but I've seen the destruction which can result from its abuse --- in my own life, as well as others.

This story is, perhaps, my favorite that I have written.

Originally published as *Behind the Door* in Hypnos Magazine (Vol. 9, Issue 2), Fall of 2020.

Godly Business

"Religion began when the first con man met the first fool." --- Mark Twain.

Godly Business is partly a) a critique on religion, b) a critique on the 'businessman mentality' and lack of ethics in the marketplace, and c) my take on the 'many-worlds interpretation' of quantum mechanics.

Quite obviously, this tale is downright weird! Hence, this story is among one of my personal favorites.

Originally published in *Penumbric Speculative Fiction Magazine*, Spring 2021.

Box of Chocolates

Ever feel impulsive and out of control? As if you don't possess more than a fraction of willpower? If so, then perhaps you can relate to this tale. Right around Valentine's Day of 2020, I sat behind the wheel of my truck, driving to the factory. My night had only begun, yet I was tired, weak, and felt a strong urge to eat my emotions. Thus, I stopped off at the Family Fresh marketplace and purchased a box of Whitman's Chocolates.

The moment I sat down in the empty factory, I devoured every last piece of chocolate with fiendish gluttony. By the time I was finished,

I felt awfully bloated and suffered a terrible belly ache.

"Never eating again," I told myself.

Out of that particular emotion, I hunkered down and wrote this story about a man who cannot control his impulsive instincts . . .

Originally published in issue #27 of *The Literary Hatchet*, summer of 2020.

The Typewriter

Once upon a time, I performed solo gigs at mid-western dive bars and cafes. I'd get up on stage (if there was a stage, otherwise I'd squeeze into a corner with my Fisherman amplifier and mic stand), strap on my guitar, set the harmonica brace around my neck, and belt out rock, folk, and blues tunes for three or four hours. This was well before my time at the factory, back when I was in my early twenties and attempting to forge a career as a musician.

On a grey, tepid afternoon in January 2019, I was driving my rusted-out Cavalier on my way to a gig. Not at a dingy dive bar crowded with drunken hooligans, but at the *Amery Classic Theater* in the quaint town of Amery, Wisconsin. Many local musicians would perform at this event, all in an attempt to raise money to repair the roof of the old theater and keep it relevant --- in the end, we weren't successful.

I used to work at a cable warehouse in Amery, and before heading to the gig I decided to park on Main Street, cross over to Birch, and see what'd become of the old warehouse which, last I'd heard, had gone under.

I was thrilled to discover the purple lettering upon the building's facade: *Vintage Thrift.*

I went inside. The old warehouse of work tables, boxes and wood pallets was now cluttered with antique items. Then, sitting upon a stand in the corner, I saw her.

A Royal typewriter, circa 1940's.

She was grey, bulky, and when I plunked down the keys, the type hands jammed. What I did next came very naturally --- I handed the nice lady at the counter $15 and hauled the immensely heavy thing into the backseat of my car.

The theater gig was fun. I read aloud two poems I'd written, sung a John Prine tune (*Fish and Whistle,* as I recall), then hopped off the stage. I stayed to watch three or four performances, then got out of there. I was eager to get home and play with my new toy.

I'd always wanted a typewriter. Now, I had one.

Gruntingly, I carried her over the threshold --- but not before ramming my shoulder into the doorframe and cursing a lot. Then I popped open the cover and began cleaning the grimy carriage house, spraying it with PB B'laster (*the #1-selling penetrant since 1957*, so I'm told).

Lesson learned, folks: always read the back of the can, especially the little fine print that instructs, *use in a well-ventilated area*. The entire house became choked with noxious fumes. Quite thankfully, my fiancé and daughter were out doing errands at the time. I feverishly opened every window in hopes of ridding the place of that horrid, thick, industrial stench.

When the girls arrived home, the first thing to come out of their mouths was, "What's that *smell?*"

I had no other choice but to admit my foolish mistake.

Finally, I sat down, replaced the dried-up ribbon with a new one which stained my fingers, then typed the first thing that came to mind:

and the slugs shall blossom.

I don't know how my subconscious came up with that line, but it struck me as creepy and I filed it away for safe keeping. Less than a month later, I'd written *The Typewriter* in its entirety. After polishing, I submitted it for an anthology about cursed items appropriately entitled, *ACCURSED: A Horror Anthology*, from Jolly Horror Press. Editor Jonathan Lambert helped me polish the tale a bit more, then purchased it for $25.

The Typewriter was my very first professional story sale, appearing in *ACCURSED* in December of 2019. I'd been writing fiction for less than a year at that point, but after ten months of rejection slips, this one acceptance was a boon to my self-esteem and gave me a glimpse of hope. For that reason, this tale remains dear to my heart.

As for my Royal typewriter, she remains well-maintenanced and is continually *click-clacking* away . . . even when my hands aren't on the keys.

When the Joke Grows Sharp Teeth

The title of this story was inspired by a wonderful documentary film entitled, *Dreams with Sharp Teeth*, about the writer Harlan Ellison.

I don't know if Harlan would've liked this story, but I'm rather pleased with it. My main objective was to show the madness and absurdity of bigotry, which I believe this story does sufficiently. Such an objective is humble, of course. It does not tackle the complex psychology of Adolf Hitler, for instance, nor does it establish any groundbreaking socio-political tract.

But, that's okay. The story works, and it *entertains*, and that's all I wanted it to do. I also think the controversial foreground, when placed against a subtext of rampant silliness, makes for a startling contrast.

The Shape

Richard Lee Morrison was --- and remains to this day --- one of my favorite people. As a young boy, my Grandfather impressed me deeply with his humor, his dignity, and his love for stories (having even written a few books of his own).

Writing *The Shape* allowed me to visit with him again, in a sense. While writing Gramps' dialogue, I was forced to reach back into my mind and recall the exact cadence and rhythm of his speech, then reproduce it as accurately and faithfully as I could onto the page. I like to think he would've been pleased with this story.

He's been gone for better than a decade, but I think about him often. I have in my possession a black suitcase containing the three novels and several short stories he'd written --- dryly humorous western stories, mostly. I have his rejection letter from Bantam Books, as well.

I look at the rejection occasionally, thinking to myself, I don't care if I get a *million* of these damned things. I'm going to keep writing, keep improving, keep pushing and hammering on that door until somebody lets me in.

With a sense of endurance, and due respect, *The Shape* was written in his memory. Love you, Grandpa. Remember what we found in the caves?

Helga's Helping Hands

I enjoy a clever alliteration, don't you? I'm hoping so. Otherwise, you probably would've picked up this book, read the title and grunted, "Geez, that sounds stupid!" before tossing it back onto the shelf with a flourish of annoyance.

We all need a helping hand, from time to time. With this tale, I wanted to write about a man so consumed by arrogance and pride that he never accepted help from anyone --- or at least, would never admit to doing so.

Consider Bernard's comeuppance at the tale's end my tribute to the gruesomely enjoyable *Tales from the Crypt* comic books of the nineteen-fifties. One of my somewhat 'moral tales', I suppose.

The Thing in Gregory Thornton's Basement

Some stories are difficult to get down. Others are a sheer pleasure to write. *Gregory Thornton's Basement* was one of the latter.

Gregory is such a malformed, weird, and unfit character, I couldn't help but shake my head and chuckle anticipating the deranged things he would do, think, or say next. The dream sequences, in particular, were a riot to compose.

I should also add that Gregory Thornton is myself, at least to some minimal extent. His gross negligence and lack of responsibility mirror my own habits from time to time. Am I as faulted and hopeless as Gregory Thornton? Far from it --- but it's in the writer's best interests to observe their own faults, magnify them, and put them on paper with a sense of style and fun. Quite reliably, this practice serves for good entertainment.

O.O.T.W

For this tale, I drew inspiration from the dirty, gritty poems of Charles Bukowski, as well as the hardboiled prose and dry witticisms of crime writer, Raymond Chandler. I wanted to create a brutal ghetto setting, wherein the more beast-like instincts of humankind are set to thrive. The inclusion of werewolves, or 'the Beast Within', is intended to blur the line between 'man' and 'beast'.

Avery's Dog

This started out being a Cujo-esque tale, but once I'd decided to include sympathetic qualities in regards to Ollie, the dog, the story grew much deeper emotionally. Is the ending predictable? Perhaps, but at least it's a happy one. As you're probably aware, most of my stories do not end on notes of absolute joy. *Avery's Dog* is the exception.

Everything is Broken

Everything is Broken, the third track on Bob Dylan's 1989 album, *Oh Mercy,* served as the initial inspiration for this tale. Folks may be surprised to hear the name Bob Dylan brought up on a list of greatest influences for a horror writer, but the man remains one of my idols. His ingenious flair for writing exceedingly visual lyrics, combined with his drawn-out phrasings and accentuations of the words (this is key, of course, *the words*) have influenced me just as much, if not more, as any writer of prose. In my humble opinion, the Nobel Prize in Literature awarded to Mr. Dylan in 2016 was well deserved.

Here, too, *The Twilight Zone* remains a vital influence upon my work. My main character (unnamed) enters a zone of existence wherein the laws of entropy reign and nothing can be built, restored, or created. There is only the slow, gradual destruction of all things and persons. The desert landscape serves as a template of desperation. Even the children born in this town of 'Broken Spring' are born broken (both in body and soul), thus cannot count as 'creations' in and of themselves.

The ending scene, of course, is tragic --- although there is some room for ambiguity. Well, what can I say? If there's one thing my readers can expect of me, it's to always end on a high note!

***

The old factory has been purchased; its fate now placed into new hands. Thus, my job here is done. I've bid my farewell to the ghosts and the rattling pipes and the mysterious groans within the walls. I've written over a hundred stories in this place. When not writing, I meditated upon each story, chewing my fingernails and slugging coffee on sunset walks around the building and the nearby streets, occasionally glancing up at the factory's singular, brick smokestack --- which, from afar, appears like a great, lonesome tower.

I've since moved on to new work, however, and the words haven't yet stopped flowing. Currently, I'm employed by Half-Price Books as a bookseller. Despite having less time to write, I'm rather fond of my new job. I enjoy stocking the shelves, promoting literacy, and helping people discover what they're looking for. On my lunch breaks, I snag an Oreo from the break room, then run out to my car and write my stories.

I write every chance I get, because I live and breathe for good stories. I adore words, you see. I'm fascinated, if not obsessed, by language and all the ways it can be utilized to focus the imagination and create stories worth reading. Hopefully you won't roll your eyes when I tell you I am a 'man of letters', but I assure you it's true. Whether or not those 'letters' are any good is another question, and not up to me to decide.

But if you were to collect the sweat from my pores, place it on a slide and put it under the microscope, you'd peer into the eye piece and see little organisms floating around . . . and they would be letters from the alphabet --- swimming, writhing, clawing. Can you picture it? Little a's and b's and c's with cyclopean eyes and tiny, gnashing teeth. And tiny though they may appear, I'll bet they're quite sharp. I'll bet they could burrow inside one's flesh . . . and *bite.*

Well, fellow friends of the macabre, I must now bring things to a close. Thank you for staying with me until the very end. I hope you've found these stories behind the stories interesting. Perhaps you'll even visit me again someday . . .

. . . even if that means you'll be going to bed with the lights on, for fear of that suddenly new, strangely contorting bundle of shadows in the corner.

Gratefully,
Tylor James.
March 9th, 2021.
From a great, lonesome tower.

THE AUTHOR

Tylor James is a horror/dark fiction writer living in the American Midwest. He's a proud member of the Horror Writers Association, and has bizarre stories featured in such publications as: *Hypnos Magazine*, *The Literary Hatchet*, *Penumbric Speculative Fiction Magazine*, *SCARE ME*, *ACCURSED: A Horror Anthology*, and *Emerging American Horror Writers: Midwest Region.*

His debut story collection, *Daydreams of the Damned: Tales of Horror & Oddity*, is available in paperback/kindle on Amazon, as is *WEIRDSMITH: Issue One*, a collection of two dynamite tales from *Too Much Weird* press.

Having committed himself long ago to writing one short story every week, Tylor keeps his head up and heart open for new ideas --- like a ravenous monster, he is perpetually hungry for them. His penchant for dark fiction has its roots in watching old horror films from an early age, and from growing up in a creepy old farmhouse in Wisconsin.

When not writing, you may find Tylor spending quality time with his fiancé and daughter, drinking gallons of black coffee, stargazing, reading a book, and/or performing as a singer-songwriter in Midwestern dive-bars. Additionally, he enjoys taking midnight strolls past the graveyard (however, he never whistles).

He is twenty-six years old.

Contact:

Facebook: Tylor James
Goodreads: Tylor James
Instagram: @tylorthewriter
Blog: tylorjames.com

Made in the USA
Middletown, DE
07 September 2024

60539773R00172